A HAND

A HANDFUL OF DREAMS

Hilary Wilde

CHIVERS
THORNDIKE

This Large Print edition is published by BBC Audiobooks Ltd, Bath, England and by Thorndike Press®, Waterville, Maine, USA.

Published in 2003 in the U.K. by arrangement with the author.

Published in 2003 in the U.S. by arrangement with Juliet Burton Literary Agency.

U.K. Hardcover ISBN 0–7540–7366–1 (Chivers Large Print)
U.K. Softcover   ISBN 0–7540–7367–X (Camden Large Print)
U.S. Softcover   ISBN 0–7862–5737–7 (Nightingale)

The text of this Large Print edition is unabridged.
Other aspects of the book may vary from the original edition.

Set in 16 pt. New Times Roman.

Printed in Great Britain on acid-free paper.

British Library Cataloguing in Publication Data available

Library of Congress Cataloging-in-Publication Data

Wilde, Hilary.
    A handful of dreams / by Hilary Wilde.
        p. cm.
    ISBN 0–7862–5737–7 (lg. print : sc : alk. paper)
    1. Inheritance and succession—Fiction. 2. Trusts and trustees—
Fiction. 3. Seychelles—Fiction. 4. Sisters—Fiction. 5. Large
type books. I. Title.
PR6072.E735H36 2003
823'.914—dc21   2003055973

CHAPTER ONE

Cilla hurried along Burford's High Street, for she mustn't be late. Aunt Lil had trained her well! Dear Aunt Lil, life would never be the same now she had died—and so suddenly, too, Cilla thought. Shivering, for it was a cold autumn day, she thrust her hands into the pockets of her green trouser suit, while her shoulder-length dark hair swung and her dark eyes were puzzled as her fingers closed round the letter in her pocket.

It was Mr Kent's letter. He was Aunt Lil's solicitor and at the funeral had told Cilla that he had some arrangements to make before he could read the will. Why was it necessary, Cilla wondered as she weaved her way in and out of the shoppers, to even read the will? They all knew what it would say.

After all, Aunt Lil only had two relations: Cilla and her sister, Joanna. Often Aunt Lil had said she felt it rather sad that there was just the three of them and that it must be fun to be part of a large family.

So it didn't make sense when Mr Kent had written:

'It has been difficult to suit us all, but please come on Friday at twelve o'clock.'

Us all? That was what didn't make sense, for there would only be herself and Mr Kent.

After all, if Joanna had not flown back from the Seychelles for the funeral, she was not likely to do so for a senseless reading of the will, as Aunt Lil had always made it clear that she would leave everything to her two nieces.

So why had Mr Kent written 'us all'?

Ahead of her Cilla saw the tall, recently-built block where Mr Kent's office was and suddenly, as if someone had switched on a light, she knew: another relation must have been found! Perhaps more than one? Certainly someone Aunt Lil had not known about. It could even be someone pretending to be a relation after having read of Aunt Lil's death and that her two nieces were the sole heiresses of her wealth. That would explain why Mr Kent had said he could not read the will at once. Obviously he had to look for other relations.

What a difference it might make. Not that she really minded. At least not for herself, Cilla thought, but she was worried about Joanna, to whom money meant so much.

In the hall, Cilla was greeted by a red-haired receptionist who had a sympathetic smile. 'It must have been a terrible shock to you when Miss Painter died,' she said.

Cilla nodded. 'I couldn't believe it. I'd seen her a few days before. I didn't even know she was ill.'

'I don't think anyone did except herself.'

'She knew?' Cilla was startled.

'She must have done, otherwise she wouldn't have altered her will.'

So new relations might have turned up before Aunt Lil died, Cilla thought. How many could there be?

Betty Armitage led the way to the inner office, opening the door. 'Miss Askew, Mr Kent,' she said.

Cilla went into the lofty room. Vaguely she noticed the red carpet, the huge window showing the cars and people outside scurrying along, but her eyes were fixed on the stranger standing by the window. He was someone she had never seen before. What was he doing there? Could he be a cousin or something?

'Come in, Cilla,' Peter Kent was saying. She turned to him, her dark hair swinging. He smiled. 'Punctual to the second. Full marks!' He was a tall lean man in his mid-forties with slightly greying hair and a friendly face. Cilla didn't know him very well, but her Aunt Lil had thought highly of him. 'I want to introduce Theo Randall,' he went on.

Theo Randall, Cilla thought. What an odd name. What relation could he be? But her thoughts came to a standstill as the man by the window turned and looked at her.

A tall man, lean but with broad shoulders. His hair was dark, inclined to be long, with sideboards, but it wasn't that that caught her eyes. It was a small curl of hair standing upon the back of his head. Her hand ached suddenly

3

to smooth it down and such an unexpected desire startled her. He was a stranger, so why . . . ?

There was something else that held her attention—his eyes. Surprisingly, with his dark hair they looked green and thoughtful, almost as if, as he was looking her up and down, he was assessing her worth. She gave a little shiver. Somehow she had a feeling he would be a difficult man to work for, a man demanding perfection and expecting it to be delivered.

He moved towards her, holding out his hand. 'We have met before, but I doubt if Cilla remembers.'

She was even more surprised. His face wasn't one you would easily forget. 'We have met?' she echoed. 'I'm terribly sorry, but—but . . .'

'You don't remember? I'm not surprised. You were very young—about six years old.'

'Was I?' It could only mean he was a relation, she thought.

'Please sit down, Cilla,' Peter Kent said as he sat down behind his broad desk and opened some papers. 'You, too, Theo.'

They both obeyed. Cilla kept glancing at the stranger, trying to think fourteen years back in an effort to remember him. That must have been about the time her mother had died.

'Now, Cilla,' Peter Kent said, looking at her worriedly, 'I'm afraid that in many ways your aunt's will is going to disappoint you and also

4

distress you very much. I can assure you I did my best to alter it. I said it was unfair, that you would be hurt . . .'

Cilla was surprised. Aunt Lil doing anything to hurt her beloved nieces? It just didn't make sense. It could only mean that Aunt Lil had left everything to this man, sitting so quietly by her side. How furious Joanna would be!

'I don't think I'll be hurt,' Cilla said slowly. 'After all, it was Aunt Lil's money and she had a right to do with it as she likes. She has always been most generous to us.'

'You were very fond of your Aunt Lil,' Peter Kent said gently.

'Of course.' Cilla closed her eyes for a moment, for the tears were near. 'She was wonderful to us.' She turned to the stranger. 'When my father died, my mother took my sister and me to live with Aunt Lil, and when my mother died, Aunt Lil . . .'

'Inherited you? I know.'

'She was wonderful. Strict maybe, but so kind.' Cilla twisted her fingers together, looking down at them, hoping the men would not see the tears in her eyes, for if they comforted her she would really cry. 'She taught us to look after ourselves, never to be dependent on anyone. That's why she made us go to London to work.'

'Your sister didn't like that. She's four years older than you?' Peter Kent asked.

'Yes. No, Joanna didn't like having to work.

5

She felt Aunt Lil was so wealthy that there was no need for us to. I think Aunt Lil was right. As she often said, you never knew what might happen, and one day we might be glad we could earn our own livings. In any case . . .' Cilla paused, afraid of what she had nearly said, but Peter Kent said it for her.

'Your aunt didn't approve of Joanna's marriage?'

'I could never understand that.'

'You liked Paul?' the stranger asked, sounding amused.

'And why not?' Suddenly she was angry. 'Just because Paul let his hair grow long and wore trendy clothes, it didn't mean he was a hippy.'

'There's no need to tell me,' Theo Randall said dryly. 'I know him.'

'You do?' Cilla stared at him. 'Then why don't I know you?'

'You did—fourteen years ago.' Again he sounded amused.

'It's a long time.'

Peter Kent intervened, 'Look, you two can fight it out later, but now there's business to be done. Please sit quietly while I read the will.' He looked at Cilla. 'I'm afraid this is going to be a shock for you.'

She smiled. 'Don't worry. Money doesn't mean anything to me. I have a good job and my dreams.'

'Dreams!' Theo Randall sounded scornful.

6

'What good do they do? Where do they get you?'

Cilla turned to glare at him. 'Life without dreams would be . . . would be in—intolerable.'

'I agree,' Peter Kent said quietly. 'Will you two please shut up?'

'Sorry,' Cilla said, and Theo Randall murmured something.

First Peter Kent spoke of the amount of money that might be left after the various taxes. Cilla stared in amazement.

'We had no idea she was so rich!'

'Wisely invested. She had good fortune and a splendid stockbroker,' Peter Kent said with a smile, but it vanished quickly as he stared at Cilla. He looked unhappy and she felt herself stiffen. Was he going to say that it had all been left to Theo Randall? How would poor Joanna react? She had always talked about the days when Aunt Lil was really old and died and they were both rich. Joanna's dreams had been of mink coats and diamonds, perhaps a yacht, a house in Miami, another in Switzerland, whereas Cilla's had been more practical—a riding school, or kennels with at least two horses and four dogs for herself!

'A yearly sum of five thousand pounds for Joanna,' Peter Kent read from the papers in his hand. Cilla knew this was because he didn't want to look at her and see the dismay he expected to be shown on her face. 'The rest of

7

the money is left to you, Cilla,' he said slowly.

'Me?' Cilla gasped. She turned to look at the man by her side. He looked back, his face grave, but he said nothing. 'But why me, Mr Kent?' Cilla turned to the solicitor imploringly. 'That isn't fair. Why leave it all to me?'

'There are certain conditions, Cilla,' he told her. 'Conditions I'm afraid you won't like.'

'I shall give Joanna her share . . .'

'That's why your aunt has made the conditions. She knew you would.'

'It's only fair. I can't hurt Joanna!' Cilla almost wailed.

The man by her side spoke quietly, but his words went home. 'You have no choice. Go on, Peter.'

'The conditions are as follows: First, that you must go immediately to the Seychelles and stay with your sister.'

'I've got to . . . ?' Cilla gasped. 'But . . . but I can't. They'll be furious. Not only with Aunt Lil but with me. I shall give Joanna her fair share,' she added defiantly.

'This is where the will steps in. You cannot spend more than a certain amount each year unless your trustees agree.'

'But that's not fair. Trustees? How could Aunt Lil do this to me?'

'That's what I said to her, but she wouldn't listen. She said you had to be protected. That, left with your share unprotected, your brother-in-law would con the lot and gamble it away.'

'Paul isn't a real gambler. Lots of people go to races.'

'But lots of people don't lose more money than they've got,' Theo Randall said quietly.

Instantly on Paul's defence, Cilla turned to him. 'He was unlucky. All his life, he's been unlucky.'

'He had good parents.'

'They weren't well off. He never had much money.'

'That was his fault, Cilla. A more lazy layabout . . .'

'Please . . . please . . . please!' Peter banged on his desk. 'Let's get on with the business.'

'I don't need a trustee,' protested Cilla.

'You have two,' Theo said with a smile. 'Peter and myself.'

'You?' Cilla was horrified. 'Then you're not . . . I thought you were a relation.'

'Good grief, no,' said Theo. 'I lived for years in the village with my grandfather, but I'm certainly no relation of yours.'

Annoyed by his amused voice, she snapped 'Thanks be! That's a relief at least.'

Peter banged on the desk again. 'Please listen, Cilla. Your aunt was afraid that you would hand over half the money to your sister.'

'Of course I will. Why not? She ought to have it.'

'She can have it. One day.' Peter Kent spoke slowly as he glanced at the papers in his hand

9

that he was using as a kind of defence. 'If you would give me a chance to talk, I can explain. The conditions have to be obeyed or else . . .'

'Or else?' Cilla echoed.

'Or else the money will be donated to various homes for cats.'

Peter Kent's voice was serious, but Cilla looked at him sharply, wondering if he was joking. Obviously he wasn't.

'But she hates . . . hated cats.'

'Maybe she feels . . . felt guilty about that hatred,' Theo by her side said quietly, his voice amused.

'Please.' Peter Kent sounded annoyed. 'I haven't got all day. I can see no reason why the conditions are unacceptable. I know they're unpleasant, but . . .'

'They'll blame me for it.'

'Perhaps they're right,' Theo Randall said.

Cilla turned, furious. 'Are you saying that I talked Aunt Lil into this . . . this unjust, mean, horrible business?'

'No, I'm not.' Theo clipped his words sharply. 'I'm suggesting that you've been a more loving, appreciative niece than your sister and that it's your Aunt Lil's love for you that's made her do this. She only wants to protect you from Paul.'

'But Paul would never . . .'

'Look, how many times must I ask you two to shut up,' Peter Kent began, but Cilla went on:

10

'How can I go out and tell them that Aunt Lil has left me so much and that I can't help them? They'll never forgive me. Isn't there any way I can?'

'You have no choice. You can tell them that,' said Theo.

'They'll hate me.'

'Of course,' he agreed calmly.

Cilla turned to Peter Kent. 'Couldn't you as trustees give me permission?'

He looked unhappy. 'It's not as simple as that, Cilla. You see, our responsibility is to protect both you and your sister. Unfortunately neither I nor Theo approve of Paul. He's got to prove to us that he's reliable and that Joanna won't suffer. If I may now speak,' he added sarcastically, 'there's more for you to know.'

'I'm sorry. I won't say a word,' Cilla promised. Peter Kent smiled. 'Take a bet on it? Your aunt has written a letter that's not to be delivered to you until the day you're married.'

'But why?'

'I don't know.' Peter Kent shrugged. 'Of course, I haven't told you perhaps the most important part of it . . .' He paused almost dramatically. 'Once you're married, Cilla, everything will be different. Your trustees can retire and you can do what you like with the money.'

'When I marry?' Cilla's voice rose. 'And suppose I don't?'

11

'Then your trustees will have to go on protecting you.'

'I can't understand it.' Cilla was nearly in tears. 'Aunt Lil was so kind, so generous, so . . . so sensible. How could she do this to me? How they'll hate me. Everyone will think . . .'

'If they think such a thing of you, Cilla,' Peter said quietly, 'they're not worth knowing. I argued with your aunt for hours, but she was obsessed with this fear that you and Joanna would suffer and Paul get all the money.'

The phone bell rang impatiently and Peter Kent answered it. He frowned as he put down the receiver. 'I'm sorry, but I've got to go. It'll be some time before all is settled, Cilla, but an advance will be paid into your bank. Come around and see me tomorrow and I'll arrange everything for your visit to the Seychelles. You'll have to ring your boss and explain the situation.'

Have I got to go . . . now?'

'Yes, at once.'

She stood up and so did the man by her side. He looked at her.

'How about having a cup of coffee with me, Cilla? As your trustee, I should be in a position to know what's best for you, and how can I do that unless I know the real *you*?' His friendly smile startled her.

'I suppose so,' she said, and Peter Kent smiled at them both as they left the room.

CHAPTER TWO

The café was packed, but somehow Theo Randall found an empty table in a small alcove that slightly shut them off from the crowd. He ordered coffee for them both and then looked at Cilla.

'Well?' he asked.

'Well?' she echoed.

He smiled. 'I thought you'd like to start. You must have a pile of questions to ask.'

She had to smile, then. 'I have. You say you knew me when I was six and that you lived in Flaxfield, but so did I and I don't remember you at all.'

'It's a long story, but it's got to be told,' Theo explained, and smiled at the waitress as she brought the coffee. 'Thanks. Like you, Cilla, I was an orphan. I lived with my grandfather in that huge hideous house on the hill—you must know it, called Riverview.'

Cilla nodded. The house was now a nursing home for the very old.

'You were living with your aunt at the time, but little more than a child. I happened to be down for the weekend after your mother died—I was at Cambridge at the time—and my grandfather was ill and asked me to represent him at the funeral. You don't remember?'

13

Closing her eyes, Cilla thought hard. She rarely thought about it, but now vaguely she remembered a gloomy day, the crowd of friends in the cottage, eating and drinking and laughing and talking, and she had suddenly realised what it all meant and that she would never see her mummy again.

'I remember crying and people saying I mustn't, that it would upset my mother, and I wondered how it could hurt her if she wasn't there,' Cilla said, shivering, opening her eyes to stare at the man sitting silently opposite her. 'I do remember. I hid in the cupboard under the stairs and someone pushed the door shut and I couldn't get out . . .'

Theo nodded. 'Exactly. You screamed and I heard you and opened the door.'

'*You* did?' Cilla sounded amazed. 'But it was an old man—I mean, you looked old.'

He smiled. 'Of course I looked old—to you. There's fourteen years between us. I was twenty and you were six. You were heartbroken. I remember how you clung to me and wept on my new shirt.' He smiled, but there was a tenderness in his voice that surprised her.

'Yes, I do remember now. How I wished you were my daddy.' Cilla laughed. 'All the girls at school had daddies and I'd always wanted one, and you . . .'

'Took you for a walk with the dog, a cairn, if I remember right, and then bought you an ice

14

cream.'

Cilla laughed. 'That was good of you.'

'You were rather a sweet kid. What about another cup of coffee? We've still got a lot to exchange.' He waved to the waitress who came immediately. 'Two more coffees, please, and what about some nice cream cakes?'

Cilla was hardly listening; she was thinking. He said: '*You were.*' Well, of course she was not a kid any more, she was twenty years and three months. That made him thirty-four.

'You said you knew Paul?' she began. If only she could convince him what a fine man Paul was!

Theo nodded. 'We were at the same school, though I'm several years older. I didn't know him well. You don't with that age gap—and even though we were in the same village for the holidays our hobbies and interests were different. His were quite definitely girls.'

'And yours?' Cilla asked, feeling a little more relaxed. Maybe Theo wasn't so difficult, maybe she would be able to persuade him?

'Drawing. Architecture. Riding. Archaeology, masses of things,' Theo told her. 'When Paul married your sister, your aunt disapproved, and I'm not surprised.'

'She never tried to stop the wedding, but she gave an amazing aura of disapproval. I could never make out, though, why she didn't like Paul,' Cilla confessed.

'You did?'

15

'Of course. I was only a kid of sixteen and I thought him smashing. He was ever so nice to me.'

'He has a charm,' Theo admitted.

'Why don't you like him?' Cilla asked bluntly.

Theo twirled a fork round on the table. 'I do and I don't. It's a strange friendship, Cilla. When they were married, he asked me to find him a job. Although I'm only an architect I know a good many people in different countries. I had just bought a *pied-à-terre*—a piece of my own land, in the Seychelles.'

'That's where they live.'

'Exactly. I got Paul the job. He's working with a well-known insurance firm. Unfortunately he's bone lazy and expects everything to be handed on a silver platter to him.'

'You must know Joanna, then?' asked Cilla, wondering why her sister had never mentioned Theo.

'Oh yes, I know her well.' Theo was smiling. 'An attractive girl, witty and a real extrovert. She's very popular on the island and has many friends. Not that I'm often there—I just go when the rat race suddenly bores me. I think you'll enjoy your visit. It's very beautiful. A thousand miles from Mombasa, in the Indian Ocean and only four degrees south of the Equator, so there's little difference in the seasons. There's a group of about eighty-five islands, many of them fascinating. Sunshine,

16

lovely beaches, calm lagoons where it's safe to swim, palm trees.' He smiled. 'A typical romantic background.'

'It won't be very romantic for me,' Cilla said bitterly. 'How can I enjoy it? And how can Aunt Lil, who was such a darling, do this to me?'

'I had the same feeling when I heard from her,' said Theo. ' I mean, quite frankly, I'd forgotten her. When my grandfather died, we sold up the house and I moved away into a different world. Then I received this letter from your aunt. I was in the Seychelles Islands at the time. Maybe Peter gave her my address, as he knew me well. Anyhow, this letter came . . .'

'Why did she write to you?' Cilla hardly heard the clatter of plates, the laughter and talking, as she leaned forward, her face grave as she tried to understand Aunt Lil's strange behaviour.

'I don't know. It seemed she'd never forgotten my kindness, as she called it, when I rescued you. Her letter was desperate, asking me to help her. She told me she knew she had only a few months to live and that she needed a man, preferably young and reliable, to help her. I must admit that I'd always liked her, despite her sharp tongue, so I came straight back to see her. I knew it was pretty urgent.'

'But if Mr Kent was a trustee . . . I mean, why bother you?'

17

'She wanted two, she said, for death lurked on the road and in the air and she wanted to be sure you were protected. She loved you very much, you know.'

Cilla looked away, her eyes smarting. Dear Aunt Lil! Life would never be the same without the small, gay little woman with her jokes, her warm welcomes, her understanding.

'She was absolutely obsessed by this fear that Paul would gamble away the lot and leave you and Joanna with nothing, so what could I do but agree?'

'I'm sorry to be such a nuisance,' Cilla began, looking at him, thinking of his busy life and now having this to think about.

'It's not your fault, but you could help by not being difficult,' he told her coldly. 'Now, I've got to be off. I'm flying back to the Seychelles tomorrow—it takes about fifteen hours—because I'm expecting my sister and her husband to stay. They have very restless feet and seem to fancy the Seychelles at the moment.'

'Was your sister living at your grandfather's?'

'No. He loathed women, of any age, so when our parents stopped fighting and both died in a car crash, I went to my father's father and Henrietta went to our mother's mother. Sounds rather involved, but it worked quite well. Peter Kent will look after you,' he added.

Taking the hint, Cilla hastily finished her coffee and followed him outside the café. Here he smiled and lifted a hand.

'I expect I'll see you out there,' he said, and left her.

Expect? Did that mean he wouldn't be there when she was? Cilla wondered. Did she mind? Would he help her, or would he be the argumentative, arrogant man he had been at the solicitor's?

CHAPTER THREE

As Cilla walked down the road she suddenly realised that there was so much to be done and so little time in which to do it, so she hurried to where she had parked her blue mini-car and drove through the town into the lovely Cotswold country towards the village where Aunt Lil's cottage was. The Cottage was a funny name, since it had five bedrooms and two bathrooms as well as a dining-room, lounge and playroom that she had had made for her nieces when they were small.

The trees were that fascinating colour of a mixture of gold and red, and Cilla wondered what sort of trees there would be in the Seychelles. Palm trees, of course, for coconuts were, apparently, their main trade. Not that Joanna had written much about the islands, not that she ever wrote much at all, to be truthful, and Cilla knew that in Joanna's four years of marriage they had grown very far apart. How would Joanna welcome her? Cilla wondered, as she drove in the curved drive round to the back of the Cottage. Would Joanna welcome her? No one could blame her if she didn't. *Would* Joanna know she could expect her sister at any moment? How long did the will say Cilla must stay out there? she asked herself. These were questions she must ask Peter Kent the next day when she saw him.

Going into the house she was greeted by Mrs Salter, the tall, thin, white-haired daily help. 'Your lunch is ready, dear. You're looking sort of sad. Nothing wrong?'

Mrs Salter had known Aunt Lil for years, so perhaps she would understand, Cilla thought, so she told the bustling sympathetic woman the whole story. Rather to Cilla's surprise, Mrs Salter didn't look shocked.

'She was always a wise one, your aunt,' Mrs Salter said as she brought in the chicken casserole. 'That Paul Beasley isn't a one you can trust.'

'Aunt Lil could have done it differently,' Cilla pointed out. ' I mean, she could have left Joanna her half and tied it up, so much to be spent each year. I felt so embarrassed. I mean, Theo Randall has enough to do without worrying about me.'

'Theo Randall!' Mrs Salter sighed happily. 'Now he was a great one. We all respected that lad. Your aunt must have died happily knowing you were under his protection. Now I'll be off. I'll pop back later this afternoon,' she finished, and was gone before Cilla could tell her not to worry. Mrs Salter still saw Cilla as the child she had first known and seemed to delight in fussing round her.

The casserole was delicious, but Cilla hardly noticed it, for she was busy thinking what she must do next. Telephone her boss—about

21

three o'clock would be best. He was a good boss, sympathetic and understanding, and she could soon be replaced. Then there was Wendy, the girl with whom she shared a flat in Gloucester Road. Well, at least, now she had so much more money, Cilla thought, she could go on paying her share of the rent until Wendy got another companion. She'd ring Wendy that evening. Then there was the Cottage to think about. Somehow she hated the idea of selling it, yet somehow she couldn't see herself living in it alone. The best thing here would be to see what Joanna said—at least the trustees couldn't stop Joanna from being Cilla's guest.

As she wandered round the Cottage, wondering what to do next, not wanting to do anything, the quiet loneliness of it seemed to haunt her. Aunt Lil's cairn had been found a home, so also had her two cats, and now there was nothing alive at all.

Mrs Salter's reaction hadn't helped Cilla to understand what her aunt had done at all, for she could only think how hurt Joanna would be, and it was a kind of insult, since Joanna was no child. Twenty-four years old and married four years, surely she had the right to do what she liked with her own money? It was as if the two trustees were going to be their enemies. There must be a way of working it, Cilla thought; suppose she pretended to buy a mink coat? Neither Peter Kent nor Theo Randall would check up and ask to see it and she could give that money to Joanna . . .

It would be rather fun, she thought for a moment. Theo Randall had made a strange impression on her—the strangest, because one moment she absolutely hated him and the next she had found herself staring at him as if mesmerised. It was absurd, but there was something about him . . .

Later that evening, going through Aunt Lil's letters and papers, sorting out her clothes that were to go to an old people's home, Cilla thought how lucky she was to have such a good boss. He had congratulated her, laughed when she said one of the conditions was to go to the Seychelles at once and said he hoped she'd enjoy herself and told her there would always be a job for her if she gambled away her heritage. He hadn't minded at all. Nor had Wendy. She had been absolutely thrilled.

'The Seychelles? Gee, you are a lucky one, Cilla! Not to worry about the flat, I'll be all right. You'll have to come up and collect your junk, but Kate, that new girl in the accounts department, is looking for somewhere, so she'll take over. How romantic!' Wendy's laugh had rung out. 'The Seychelles and one of the wealthiest men in London as a trustee!'

'Is he?' Cilla had asked, startled.

'Don't you ever read the gossip columns in the papers, Cilla?' Wendy had asked with a laugh. 'They're always getting at Theo Randall. A wealthy bachelor of thirty-four,

23

who spends his time deftly eluding the predatory females—and here you are, tied up with him. Your aunt was a clever one.'

'I don't understand,' Cilla had told her. 'I didn't know he was rich, or even that he existed.'

'You're way behind the times,' Wendy had teased. 'Well, good luck, and don't forget to write to me. You'll be up one day soon to collect things?'

'Yes, I'm seeing the solicitor again tomorrow and then I'll be up. See you!'

Now, sitting alone in the empty house, Cilla remembered Wendy's words : 'Your aunt was a clever one.'

Could Theo have thought the same?

Oh, no! That would be intolerable. And it wasn't true. Aunt Lil was never a match-maker, indeed she didn't believe in young marriages. Thirty was a sensible age, she had always said. But Theo might not know this—he might think . . .

The very idea made Cilla squirm.

Next day she asked Peter Kent what he thought. He laughed.

'Your aunt still saw you as a child. I'm sure she had nothing of that nature on her mind. She used to say she wondered what you would do with your money. She thought you'd buy several horses, but you'd need another house, as the Cottage is without a paddock.'

'I'd be able to afford another house with a

groom and some gardeners and . . .' Cilla began, her eyes half-shut.

'You were talking about dreams yesterday!'

Cilla looked up. 'And Theo Randall said they were no help at all. I don't agree.'

'Neither do I. What, exactly, are your dreams?'

Cilla half closed her eyes again and thought. 'A big, but not too big house with stables and a garage and big paddocks. Maybe I'd have a lot of horses and run a riding school. Or keep kennels. I love dogs.'

He smiled. 'You don't have to work, you know. You've more than enough money to live on.'

'I can't imagine doing nothing all day. Can you?'

Laughing, he agreed that he could not. Then they got on to business. He had already arranged for her ticket. She would be flying to the Seychelles in four days' time. 'Don't worry about the Cottage at the moment. You may come back with different views and decide to keep it. Mrs Salter will look after it and prices are going up fast, so you might benefit by waiting. Well, you've got a lot to do and so have I . . .' he finished as he stood up.

It was only as she drove back to the Cottage that Cilla realised she had forgotten to ask him how long the condition said she must stay in the Seychelles. She would ring Peter up to find out, she thought, as she looked up at the lovely hills and the beautifully green grass, and the autumn-kissed leaves that were fluttering down all the time to cover the ground.

* * *

She didn't remember that question until she was sitting in the plane, waiting for the take-off. There had been so much to do in a short time that it had seemed madly muddling and she had hardly known where she was. But at least she was on her way. Wendy had come to see her off, but now Cilla was alone. It was not the first time she had flown, as she and Aunt Lil had quite often gone abroad for holidays together. That had been a big help, Peter had said, as Cilla's passport and vaccination certificate were up to date. And now here she was. The plane was gradually filling up. She had an end seat by a window, but unfortunately it looked out on the wings of the plane, so she couldn't hope to see much. Just as everyone seemed to have settled down, the hostess, very pretty in her smart uniform, her cap tilted on her honey-brown hair, brought a young boy with her.

'He's travelling alone,' she said to Cilla. 'Mind if he sits next to you?'

'Of course not,' Cilla said quickly. 'I'm alone, too.'

The boy looked about twelve years old. One day he would be handsome, Cilla thought, as she introduced herself and learned that his name was Anthony Harding, that he was going to the Seychelles to his parents. He talked easily, as if used to grown-ups.

'My mum and dad are a restless sort, always moving around. They said that while I was in boarding school in England, they could go round the world. Well, they have been, and it's time we had a home.' There was a wistfulness in his face as he looked at Cilla. 'I'd like a horse and a dog and . . .'

'So would I,' Cilla said warmly. 'I love horses. Can you ride?'

There were fifteen hours of flying, broken up by well-served meals as well as drinks, plus a wearisome time when the lights went out and she tried to sleep, her head lolling painfully, waking her up each time she fell asleep. Anthony was a real help, for they talked a lot, even played noughts and crosses, and he taught her a card game which he always won, much to his delight, also they both drew pictures, Anthony showing intense interest in drawing warships of the days when men shot with arrows.

As the plane landed on Mahé Island, Cilla thanked her companion.

'I really enjoyed that,' she said with a smile.

He smiled back. 'So did I. Ever so.'

As they made their way across to the Customs and Immigration it was delightfully hot, the sun shining from a cloudless sky, and

27

Cilla glanced down at him. 'You are being met?'

'Oh yes,' he said proudly. 'My mum will be here.' He looked up. 'Are you being met?'

'I imagine so.' For the first time on the flight, Cilla remembered that a far from warm welcome might be awaiting her. Peter Kent had said he had sent Joanna a copy of the will, so she would know all that. He had also sent a cable, saying when Cilla's plane would arrive. 'Yes, I'm sure I will be,' she added.

There were quite a lot of passengers and even more people to welcome them crowded round a barrier. After Cilla had been through the usual formalities, she went out into the hall and looked around. She couldn't see either Joanna or Paul, so she sat down on a seat to wait. Gradually the passengers and their welcoming friends and relations vanished and she saw that she was alone—and then realised she wasn't, for sitting on a seat the other side of the room was Anthony Harding. Cilla went over to him.

'Hasn't your mum come?' she asked.

He shook his head. 'Hasn't your sister?'

'No. Maybe they're ill or had a puncture or something,' Cilla said as she sat down.

He looked up. 'Maybe they've forgotten,' he said wistfully.

Normally Anthony was so full of self-confidence that it was his rare bits of wistfulness that Cilla noticed so much. Oddly they reminded her of Theo Randall and his occasional moments of tenderness that had surprised her so.

Cilla and her new friend waited and talked, but it seemed hours. In the end, they got a cold drink and tried to hide their feelings. Cilla had an uncomfortable one that this was Joanna's way of showing her fury at the will. Joanna had always had a quick temper—but would Paul have let her do such a mean thing? Perhaps he was the one to meet her and was deliberately making her wait as a form of punishment.

Anthony began to get restless, suggesting that they might be in the wrong part of the building. It was then that Cilla realised that Joanna might not have got the cable. You never knew what happened in these far distant places.

'I'm going to try to get a taxi, Anthony,' she said, 'and go out to my sister. She may not even know I'm coming, as letters and things can get lost. That may have happened with your mother. Why not come with me? I can leave a message at the reception desk and when your mother gets here, she'll ask and they'll tell her where you are. You can't just wait here . . . all alone . . .' As Cilla spoke, she looked up and saw a girl walking by them, staring at them as if curious—a tall girl with blonde hair and wearing a green dress.

'Come on, Anthony,' Cilla said, and led the way to the reception desk.

There she was told they would send for a taxi. She gave them her sister's address and they said they would look out for Anthony's mother.

'If we see someone looking around, we'll let her know where you are,' a plump friendly woman said with a smile at Anthony.

The taxi came with a Creole driver who was all smiles as he fetched their luggage. Anthony scrambled in, looking quite interested as they drove along the coast.

Even with the uncomfortable wonder of what sort of welcome lay ahead of her, Cilla could not fail to see the beauty of everything. The different colours of the sea—azure blue and turquoise; the coconut palms that grew up on the side of the great mountain that towered above them; the glimpses of white beaches as the car went weaving along the coast. There were houses here and there, some quite large with wide verandahs, others small and huddled together. She saw small sweet-sounding waterfalls as the water came down the side of the mountain—and newly washed clothes spread out on bushes at the side of the rivers. They saw gardens bright with the most gorgeous flowers—red, yellow, blue, every shade, and the purple-flowered creepers that seemed to be everywhere, winding round trees or houses.

'It's so beautiful . . .' Cilla said slowly, wondering why Joanna had never said so. In

30

her letters, she had always been rather critical: too much rain, heavy winds, the mosquitoes she loathed and that kind of complaint. Yet this beautiful . . .

Cilla looked round at the lovely palm trees bending over the water—at the small boats out at sea where the waves came pounding in at the reefs. The most amazing thing was surely the enormous rocks, many of them looking like caricatures of people or animals, balanced so precariously as if they were ballet dancers on their toes.

'It's all right, I suppose,' shrugged Anthony, looking up at the mountain. 'I wonder where one can ride.'

'There must be places. Has your father got a house here?'

Anthony looked surprised. 'They won't ever buy a house, they say. We're staying with my uncle.'

'You don't know his address?'

'I don't know him.'

'Never mind. They must be expecting you, so they're sure to go along to the airport,' Cilla was saying, and the car turned off the main road and down what looked like little more than a track, winding round groups of palm trees and giving glimpses of the sea.

Suddenly they came out into the open and there ahead of them was a beautiful lagoon, surrounded by tall, balanced, pointed rocks while the huge waves outside burst into scores

31

of tiny balloons as the water was tossed in the air when it met the rocks. She turned her head as the car stopped and saw that they had reached Le Bret, Joanna's home.

It was a white house with a wide verandah. Only one floor, the beautiful purple flowers growing over the walls and French windows leading to the house. The garden was wonderful, a wide beautifully cared-for lawn and flowers everywhere and of every colour. How could Joanna have lived here and not written to tell them how unutterably beautiful it was? Cilla wondered.

The Creole driver was out of the car, getting out the luggage. Cilla suddenly realised she should have changed her English money to the local coinage at the airport, but the Creole smiled and spoke English quite well, seeming more than satisfied in taking English money.

When he had driven off, Cilla looked at the house. Surely if Joanna was in, she would have heard the car? But no one had come. The house looked closed, as if shutting her out.

'Where's your sister?' Anthony asked, staring up into a tree that leaned over the lawn. He grabbed Cilla's arm and said excitedly : 'Look—there's a monkey!'

And so there was—his little white face peering down through the fernlike leaves of the palm tree before he swung away and vanished.

'I like monkeys,' Anthony said.

At that moment two Afghan hounds came running round, with their long silky coats and their graceful movements. Anthony was immediately bending down to stroke them, but Cilla realised they could not just stand in the garden for ever, so she went to the French windows and saw a bell. She pressed it. Again and again and again . . .

Through the glass she saw Joanna coming, yawning, rubbing her eyes sleepily, wearing a pale yellow dressing-gown, her red hair just as lovely as it always had been.

Joanna opened the door. 'Why, it's you!' she said in a surprised voice. 'I thought Paul was going to meet you.'

Was he, Cilla wondered, or was this their way of greeting her, making it plain that she was very unwelcome? Not that she blamed them. If she had been Joanna, and with Joanna's dreams, Cilla knew she could have been angry, too.

Then Joanna saw Anthony. 'Who on earth . . . what . . .' she began, and at that moment another car came driving in to park outside the house.

Cilla stared and caught her breath. It was Theo Randall!

CHAPTER FOUR

As Theo walked towards them, Joanna's face brightened.

'Why, Theo, what a treat!' she called delightedly.

Cilla said nothing; she moved a step back, as Theo was not looking at her. He went straight to the boy, holding out a hand.

'Hi, Anthony, I'm your Uncle Theo,' he said. Anthony shook hands solemnly. 'Where's Mum and . . . and Dad?'

Theo laughed. 'Yours is as good a guess as mine, son. I heard from your ma that you would be coming out, but she didn't say which day or when. I wouldn't have known, but a friend of mine saw you at the airport and then phoned me.' He laughed. 'She was quite hysterical.' He looked at Cilla. 'She thought you were kidnapping the lad.'

'Are you suggesting . . .' Cilla began indignantly, then stopped, for Theo was no longer paying any attention to her. He had turned to Joanna.

'Why weren't you at the airport?' he asked, his voice casual, yet it had a stabbing, tell-me-the-truth kind of accent.

'Paul said he'd go. I had a migraine,' Joanna told him.

Cilla half-closed her eyes. The old story!

34

Whenever there was anything Joanna had not wanted to do, she had a convenient migraine. She was still using it, then.

Theo was now talking to his nephew. 'Last time I heard from them they were in Kenya but on their way here, so they may turn up at any moment. Come along back with me.'

'Have you a horse?' Anthony asked. 'And a dog?'

Theo smiled. 'I have six horses and four dogs.' Anthony's face became radiant. 'Goody!' he grinned happily.

Cilla did not move. So Theo actually *had* what her dream was! It was just as if she was not there, the way they were ignoring her. She felt inclined to collect her luggage and go to Victoria, the capital of the island. Yet she couldn't do that. Unless Joanna and Paul actually threw her out, she had to stay. Maybe it would be better for the cats' homes to have the money. It seemed that money caused so much unhappiness, so much envy and jealousy, and she didn't really need it. She had a good job.

Her thoughts were interrupted by Theo. 'Look Cilla, I need your help,' he said. 'Also we have much to discuss. I'll send the car over for you in the morning, about ten.' He turned to smile at Joanna and although Cilla had thought he had a face it would be hard to forget, now she saw just how good-looking he was, in a strong way with a squarish chin—but, she noticed with a sudden little moment of amusement, that curl was still standing up on the back of his head.

'I know our Joanna never gets out of bed until about twelve o'clock,' Theo went on, 'so she won't miss you. See you then, Cilla. Come along, Anthony. Maybe we'll be hearing from your mum. She's much fonder of phones than of writing letters.'

'You're telling me,' Anthony said with a strange adult air. 'They got mad about it at school. I didn't mind, but the Head did and it made it hard at times.'

'Goodbye, then,' Theo said cheerfully, and he and the boy walked to the car. Cilla felt like rushing after them, grabbing Theo's arm, asking him to stay and back her up during the next few hours. She dreaded them. She could tell Joanna was angry—she had always had that kind of lilt in her voice when she was.

After the car had gone there was a strange silence—Joanna, in her dressing-gown that was pretty enough to be any dress, and Cilla, tired, nervous, very uncomfortably hot in the warm trouser suit that the cold autumn wind of England had made her wear when she left.

The silence seemed to go on for hours as neither moved and Cilla's luggage lay on the path. Then Cilla made a move.

'I'm sorry, Joanna,' she said.

Joanna's eyes flashed. 'I should think so, too! I've never been so shocked or hurt in my life. When we heard Aunt Lil had died, it seemed the chance of a lifetime. Paul and I planned what we would do—travel round the world, meet all the big noises, perhaps be invited on a yacht in the Mediterranean. We had such dreams, and now . . .' she added bitterly.

'I know. It must have been a shock, it was to me.'

'Was it?' Joanna asked.

Cilla's cheeks burned. She had been waiting for this.

'Do you honestly think I had anything to do with it?'

Joanna shrugged, turning away. 'Who knows? Well, we'd better go in. I was resting—this wretched migraine.'

'I'm sorry to disturb you,' Cilla began stiffly.

Joanna swung round. 'You have no choice, nor have we. Anything is better than the lot going to the cats. How could Aunt Lil do that to us, Cilla? Especially when she hates cats.'

'That's what I couldn't understand,' confessed Cilla.

'Come inside. Your room is ready,' Joanna led the way.

It was a beautiful house—surprisingly lofty rooms, each with enormous picture windows and a verandah outside. The furniture was modern, the oil paintings on the wall were abstract, the curtains pure silk and bright colours, golden and deep purple.

Joanna led the way through the large room into a corridor. At the end, she opened a door. 'This is yours,' she said, her voice cold.

Cilla stood still, looking round. 'It's lovely,' she said.

The curtains were an apricot-coloured silk with a matching bedspread, the floor was highly polished with several yellow rugs. There was an armchair, a desk and a chair, a huge wardrobe built in, a dressing table with a long mirror. But it was the brightness that fascinated Cilla, the view through the window of the grass lawn going down towards the white sand and the blue lagoon. There were birds darting about the garden, with bright yellow beaks and deep red breasts.

'It really is lovely,' she said again.

Joanna shrugged. 'You can't live on scenery. One can get awfully bored here. My Henrietta should be around, she's apt to fall asleep when not working. Are you hungry?'

'I am a bit,' Cilla confessed.

'You'd probably like a bath, so I'll leave you. She'll bring in your luggage, the bathroom is next door. I'll see you in half an hour.'

'Okay,' said Cilla, trying to sound cheerful.

In fact, she was feeling more depressed each moment that passed. Joanna obviously blamed her for what had happened. Cilla knew her visit would be a miserable one. Surely Aunt Lil could have known that, too?

A slim dark girl came in with a smile that

seemed to fill her face as she carried in the luggage and started to unpack.

'It's all right,' Cilla said quickly, 'I can do it.'

The girl gave what looked like a little curtsey and a smile and left her. Cilla had the bath running as she hastily unpacked. She hadn't brought much out with her, for she had very few thin clothes, the kind Peter had said she would need. There must be shops somewhere near so she could buy something more suitable.

After the bath and brushing her hair, she put on a thin white dress and went to the large lounge. There was no one there, but Henrietta came hurrying, giving her funny little curtsey and saying in her broken English that the food, it was ready. She took Cilla to an equally large room; the dining-room, with a huge oval table and about ten chairs round it, as well as deep blue curtains and pale blue wallpaper. It looked as if Paul and Joanna did a lot of entertaining, Cilla thought as she sat down.

'Madame?' she asked.

'She is not one to eat—in the day,' Henrietta said slowly.

So Cilla was alone—with cold meat and salad. How quiet it seemed, she thought, how strange with Henrietta standing behind her chair patiently. But at last the meal was over, the chocolate mousse being delicious, and Cilla wondered what she should do next. It was obvious that Joanna didn't want to talk to her, and yet they must. They could not live together even for a few weeks, unless they were able to talk.

CHAPTER FIVE

Joanna was waiting on the verandah, sitting comfortably with her legs up on a garden swinging chair. She was wearing a leaf-green dress that made the redness in her hair even more beautiful.

Joanna had always been the beauty, the lively niece with the friends she brought . to the Cottage, whereas Cilla had been the quiet, ordinary-looking girl with few but very good friends, a happy girl, whereas Joanna had never been content, her dreams always demanding more that she had. Cilla realised all this as Joanna called. Her legs felt reluctant to move her, but she went out into the sunshine with the beautiful view before her. She was in no mood for admiring the view; she was trying to face up to what she knew lay ahead.

Looking up at her, Joanna began. 'I didn't know you knew Theo,' she said, her voice almost accusing.

Taken aback, for she had expected a very different kind of remark, Cilla said, 'I only met him the other day. I didn't know you knew him, either.'

'Paul was at the same school,' Joanna explained.

'I know. Theo told me.' Cilla sat down in a

41

chair near her sister. 'Look, Joanna, we've got to get this clear. I knew nothing about Aunt Lil's will. You must believe me. It was as great a shock to me . . .'

Joanna gave an odd smile. 'If you say so.'

'You don't believe me, do you?' Cilla drew a long deep breath. 'Look, you must believe me, Joanna. When Mr Kent called me to his office to hear the will read, I thought it was a waste of time, because Aunt Lil had always said we were the only two in her family, so why was there the need for a will or the reading of it? Then I thought maybe they had found a relation, or several, but when Peter Kent read out the will, it was a terrible shock, and I said at once I would give you half the money. Then . . . then I heard the conditions and I couldn't believe it.'

'Nor could I,' Joanna said bitterly. 'I thought Aunt Lil loved me.'

'She did—that was one of the reasons . . .' Cilla began quickly, and paused. How could she tell Joanna that Aunt Lil had not trusted Paul?

Apparently there was no need to, for Joanna said at once, 'She hated Paul. She just hated him, and it wasn't fair. It wasn't his fault his father married another woman . . .'

'His father . . . married another . . .' began Cilla curiously.

'Yes.' Joanna's eyes were bright with anger. 'It was all so unfair. I didn't know. Aunt Lil

42

never suggested that she had ever been in love. It was Paul's mother who told him. Aunt Lil and Paul's father were engaged. The marriage was only a week away when he eloped with her best friend. Aunt Lil never forgave him. That's why she hated Paul, their son, and why she didn't want me to marry him—why she's behaved so meanly. How do you think Paul feels? Why should he—and I—be punished for something his father did? In any case, I can't see Aunt Lil being a loving little wife, she was far too bossy.'

Aunt Lil? Cilla was thinking. In love and never able to forget the pain she felt when she was rejected? Could it be true? It didn't seem so to her, for Aunt Lil had never been bitter or the kind of woman who never forgave. Yet, in a way, it explained things—and yet in another way it didn't, for why should she hurt Cilla for something Paul's father had done? No, it was more likely something Paul's mother had made up, for it had been obvious to everyone in the village that Aunt Lil and Mrs Beasley were not good friends.

Joanna was still talking and Cilla made an effort to jerk back to the present and listen. It was the same thing over and over again—how could Aunt Lil be so cruel, so mean, so unfair, about the disappointment Paul and Joanna had felt, the injustice? Wasn't there a way out?

'I said at once I'd give you half,' Cilla managed to get a word in, 'and that was when

Peter Kent said there were the conditions. I had to come out here at once and I mustn't spend more than a certain amount of money each year without one of the trustees' approval.'

'Trustees?' echoed Joanna. 'Mr Kent said nothing about that, just that he was a trustee. Who's the other?'

'Theo.'

'Theo?' Joanna was so startled that she sat up, nearly falling off the swinging chair. 'Where does he come into it?'

Cilla hesitated. How could she say frankly to her sister that Aunt Lil had believed Paul would gamble away all the money?

'She felt there should be two trustees in case one got killed.'

'But it's absurd! You're no child. You don't need protecting—and against whom? Paul, I suppose,' Joanna said bitterly. 'What have the trustees got to do?'

'I'm only allowed so much money each year,' Cilla explained. 'If I want more than that—which I would want if I could have it—I have to have one of the trustees' permission.'

'Only one?' Joanna's face brightened. 'That's not so bad, then. Theo is a very close friend of mine. I'm sure I can make him see . . .' She actually smiled. 'Oh, that does make things better.'

A long white car turned into the drive. Joanna waved.

'Here's Paul,' she said, then turned to Cilla. 'He's terribly jealous of Theo and most possessive. I don't want him to know Theo is mixed up in all this if we can possibly avoid it.'

'Won't Theo tell him?' asked Cilla.

'I'll ask him not to mention it.' As Paul came in Joanna's voice changed. 'I still think you must have known something about it, Cilla.'

'I didn't . . .' Cilla began, startled by the sudden attack as Paul came through the French window.

'Why, Cilla, nice to see you. My, how you've changed in the last four years,' he said as he pulled her to her feet and kissed her.

Paul had changed, too, she was thinking. He was still short, but now he was much fatter. His hair was sandy, still long to his shoulders. He was wearing a thin suit and seemed really pleased to see her.

' 'I'm four years older,' Cilla said with a laugh. 'No longer a teenager.'

'A very much prettier one. I'm sorry I couldn't meet you. I got held up by the boss and when I eventually got to the airport they said they'd got you a car. Well, how are things?'

'She says she's very upset about it all,' said Joanna.

Paul hugged Cilla. 'Of course she is—so are we all, but let's face it, it was the old lady's money, so she had a right to do with it as she

45

likes.'

'We *are* her flesh and blood,' Joanna objected.

'Let's forget it,' shrugged Paul. 'Now, sit down, Cilla, and tell me all the news. Are you selling the Cottage?'

'I wanted to talk to you both about it. I don't want to live in it alone.'

'I don't want to live in it—ever,' said Joanna. 'But if you sell it—can you give me half?'

'If the . . .' Cilla began, but Joanna butted in 'If the trustee agrees, you can?'

'Yes.' Cilla was puzzled. Why mustn't Paul know Theo was a trustee—and why was he jealous of Theo? Could Theo and Joanna be in love? Theo had said she was attractive and witty and it was obvious that Joanna thought a lot of him, too.

Paul laughed. 'Poor little Cilla! For the rest of your life you've got to do what the trustee says.'

'No, I haven't,' Cilla said quickly, relieved that Paul was there, for already the atmosphere had changed. He didn't believe that she had known anything about the will—nor did he blame her for it. How very different from her own sister's attitude. 'When I get married, I can do what I like. There'll be no . . . no trustee to approve of what I want or disapprove.'

'When you marry?' Paul said with a smile.

46

'Then you won't have to put up with it for long. A girl like you won't stay single.' He jumped up. 'Feel like a walk? I do, and it would do the dogs good.' He laughed. 'No use asking Joanna. She won't walk an inch more than she can help.'

'I should have a car—cooped up here all day long,' complained Joanna.

Cilla's eyes brightened. 'Couldn't I buy a car, then you could borrow it?'

Joanna sat up, her face bright with delight. 'Now that really is a good idea. You drive? A pity.' She shrugged. 'Still, we can share it.'

'Yes. It must . . .' Again Cilla hesitated, for Paul might say that on the island she could do what she liked when she was so far from her trustee, not knowing that one of them lived so near.

Paul was looking at her shoes. 'Got some flat heels? It's quite a climb. Got a hat? You haven't? Well, there's a straw one somewhere. I'll find it.' He hurried inside the house.

Joanna beamed. 'Bless you, Cilla! I've wanted a car of my own for years.'

'We'll have to pretend it's mine,' said Cilla. 'Theo . . .'

'Don't worry about him,' Joanna said, waving her hand theatrically. ' He'll look the other way all right. Better go and change your shoes. Sooner you than me!' she laughed.

Paul was waiting when Cilla returned, her shoes changed. He tossed her a cream straw

47

hat with a pointed peak and a red ribbon tied round it, with two strips of ribbon hanging behind. The dogs came racing to join them when Paul whistled, so elegant and graceful, so happy.

'Joanna hates walking,' Paul explained as they walked down the track, the dogs racing ahead then running back to leap up at them joyously.

'She always did,' Cilla said with a laugh.

'She hates everything but money,' Paul went on as they crossed the main road and began to walk up a winding path that went through the palm trees.

Cilla looked at him quickly. ' I'm afraid she always had a thing about money.'

'Yes, she's always pushing me, wanting me to be ambitious. But I'm afraid I'm made the way I am.' He sounded so sad Cilla felt she had to comfort him.

'It's a nice way, so I wouldn't worry,' she told him.

He put his arm lightly round her shoulders. 'Bless you! I sometimes wonder why she married me. She should have waited for someone like Theo—someone born rich, inheriting a fortune and making one. He knows all the right people—that's why he's such a success as an architect. The main thing is always to know the right people.'

The path had narrowed, so now he took his arm away and walked ahead, talking over his

48

shoulder. Rex and Rue, the dogs, had raced on ahead of them. It was strangely quiet, but every now and then a brightly coloured bird would swoop down on them and sing, soon to be joined by another and then another. There were butterflies everywhere, a size Cilla had never seen before and such wonderful colours.

It was a long climb and Cilla began to wish she hadn't agreed, because she was growing more and more sleepy. The humidity made it hard to breathe as they clambered over fallen stones or roots of the palm trees. As they moved into a flat opening, a group of yellow-headed birds appeared, all chattering away.

Paul looked back. 'Time we got back. The mynahs always do that as a warning that the sun is thinking of setting. But first come and see this view.'

His hand on hers, he took her over the uneven surface—for they were now standing on top of a huge stone—to the edge. It was terrifying—a deep drop, an absolute drop of the height they had climbed. At the bottom was a churning pool of water which was fed by lots of little waterfalls.

For a moment, Cilla felt frightened, for it was as if it was enticing her and she was glad of Paul's hand as she stepped back quickly.

'You don't like heights?' he asked with a smile.

'Not . . . . not if there's nothing in front of me,' she confessed.

He laughed. 'It sort of calls you, doesn't it? I think it would be an easy way to die.'

Cilla turned, her face shocked. 'You're not . . . ?'

'Thinking of suicide?' He sighed. 'No. Sometimes I do. Much as I love Joanna, there are times when she drives me nuts. She wants so much and I can give her so little.'

'You give her love,' Cilla said gently.

'Does she want it?' he asked bitterly. 'Sometimes I wonder. There's no satisfying your sister. Give her what you can and she still wants more.'

'Five thousand pounds a year is a lot of money,' Cilla pointed out.

'Not to Joanna. Fifty thousand pounds a year would be nearer her mark,' he said bitterly. 'She wants the impossible.'

'She always did,' sighed Cilla.

They were making their way slowly down the path, Cilla grateful for Paul's hand on her arm as the ground was slippery and she kept giving little skids.

'Look, Paul,' she said, 'we'll think up a way to do it. So long as it seems I'm spending the money on myself, I can spend a lot on Joanna. That might help.'

He turned his head and she was startled to find it so near hers. She could feel the warmth of his breath as he smiled.

'Bless you, Cilla! You're a darling.' They were within sight of the house when he

50

suddenly turned, his face startled. 'What happens when you die, Cilla? Will it all go to a cats' home?'

'I never thought of that,' she confessed. 'I should think my nearest relative—which is Joanna—would get it. I'll ask . . .' She stopped just in time. She had so nearly said *Theo*—and that was the last thing she must do. 'When I write to Peter Kent, I'll ask him,' she finished.

Paul laughed. 'Not that it matters. You're good for another seventy years, I'd say.'

'Help!' she laughed. 'I don't think I want to live that long.'

He looked at her strangely. 'It all depends, doesn't it?' There was an odd expression in his eyes she could not understand.

But she could agree. What he meant was that it all depended on happiness, and how could you be happy when you were alone? As she was alone now. Joanna had Paul. Theo had Anthony. She had no one. No one at all.

CHAPTER SIX

It was like living in a fairy tale, Cilla thought, when she went to bed that night. After drinks, they had had a delicious dinner and some neighbours had dropped in for the evening, to play bridge. As Cilla did not play, it gave her a good excuse to slip away and go to bed early, for she was desperately tired.

And worried. When the neighbours, a couple, came in and Joanna had introduced her, the wife had said: 'So *you're* the sister, are you?' in a very odd sort of voice that had made Cilla's cheeks burn and Paul rush to her rescue.

'Yes, she's Joanna's kid sister. When I last saw her she was still at school.'

The conversation had become general, but Cilla could not forget the emphasis on the words: 'the sister'. Had Joanna told all her friends? Did everyone believe that Cilla had played up to her aunt in order to get all the money? Cilla could not help feeling that the two neighbours had looked at her with curious and condemning eyes.

Who could blame them? she asked herself, as she paced the room miserably, pausing every now and then by the window to draw back the curtain and look at the lovely silver line that was the reflection of the moon on the sea—and the beauty of the palms silhouetted against the star-spangled sky.

Indeed, who could blame them, she thought, for it must seem awful—the young sister getting everything while the older one only got a yearly allowance. Cilla wondered how she could convince them all that she didn't *want* the money, she would have been far happier could she have given half to Joanna. Or even all of it, for that matter, she thought miserably.

Finally she went to bed, and lay back against the pale pink pillows, looking round the beautiful room, wishing with all her heart that she had Aunt Lil to write to to tell her of the beauty of it all. Of course she could write to Wendy, but somehow she didn't think Wendy would be interested in the beautiful garden, the lovely house, the wonderful ocean, the mountain that was so stately and yet, in a way, so menacing, and the gracious life of having everything done for you, and done so well. Cilla smiled as she remembered the small flat she and Wendy had shared happily, the little annexe of a kitchen, the problem of throwing away the rubbish, the steep stairs they had to run up to reach the flat. This was so completely, so utterly different.

She could hear the laughter coming along the verandah—the voices. All four of them had someone who cared. Now that Aunt Lil had gone . . .

Finally she slept, to awake to an amazing sight—the sun pouring through the window, the sea turned into a mass of glorious gold. Henrietta brought her a cup of tea and asked what she would like for breakfast.

'An egg? Is it hard or soft?' Henrietta asked. Hard or soft? Oh, boiled, of course! Cilla thought, and smiled.

'Soft, please.'

Henrietta gave a little bob and left her. Cilla bathed, then studied her small wardrobe of clothes that looked lost in the huge cupboard. The dress she had worn the day before had vanished, hanging over Henrietta's arm, obviously to be washed and ironed. Cilla finally decided on a pale yellow dress and carefully brushed her hair, wondering why she bothered as she made up her face. Theo had so many beautiful women who all rushed at him, according to Wendy, that he was not likely to look at—even less to *see*, the girl he had called a sweet kid when she was six years old.

How quiet the house was, she thought, as she ate her breakfast alone. Paul must have gone off to work and Joanna didn't get up until twelve o'clock. What a strange way to live, Cilla thought, yet in this hot humid air, her lethargic limbs had to be forced to move and she was already beginning to see why people appeared lazy. It was hard to feel or be energetic. Perhaps in time . . .

But how long must she stay? She crossed her fingers; she must try to remember to ask Theo how long she had to stay. Somehow after last night and the neighbours' attitude, she rather dreaded meeting any more of Joanna's friends.

She was sitting on the verandah when the car came—a long green car. She watched as a man got out, obviously the chauffeur, in white uniform. He hurried round the back of the house and in a few moments Henrietta came, giving her little bob. 'The car, it is here.'

'Mr Randall's?' Cilla asked.

Henrietta smiled and bobbed again. 'Yes, *mademoiselle*, it is.'

Cilla took the hat she had worn the day before and her handbag and went out into the hot sunny air. She drew a deep breath, for there was a strangely sweet smell she wondered from what flower it came.

The Creole opened the door and waited politely until she was settled. He drove carefully while Cilla looked round with what she realised were almost hungry eyes. Each thing she saw was more beautiful than anything she had ever seen before. There were small bungalows with tiny private coves in front of them, gardens filled with flowers, and always the palm trees, many bent almost double as they had been pushed in the heavy winds. It didn't take long before they were driving up a narrow avenue of tall trees whose branches met overhead so that the sunshine could only peep through the leaves, and then she saw Theo's house.

She caught her breath with amazement. It was the sort of house that she had always had in one of her dreams. It had begun years ago at school when the class had been told to draw the house they would like to live in. Much as she loved the Cottage, she had not drawn that. Instead she had drawn a house that was like the letter E without the middle short line, a longer building with a shorter one at each end and in the centre a garden, filled with flowers. And Theo's house was exactly like that! What a coincidence—it seemed impossible, yet it was true.

As the car stopped, Theo came out to meet her. His pale blue shirt was open at the neck and matched the shorts he wore.

He smiled. 'You survived?' he asked.

As she got out of the car, she looked at him. 'Just—thanks to Paul.'

There were two deck chairs on the lawn, under a huge red and white sunshade. 'Sit down,' he said. 'We're waiting for Anthony.'

'Where is he?' she asked.

'Gone for a ride with one of my men. He says you ride?'

She nodded. 'I love it.'

'Good. My horses need exercising. We must arrange something. Look,' his voice changed as it so often did, losing the friendliness,

56

becoming hard and demanding, 'Joanna rang me up and asked me not to let Paul know I was one of the trustees. Is this your idea?'

'Of course it isn't. Why should I mind? It was her idea.'

'It was? Then why? There must be a reason,' he snapped at Cilla, almost as if she was to blame.

'She says Paul is jealous of you.'

Theo laughed, a strange, not-amused-at-all laugh. 'He has been from the day we met. He was jealous because I lived in the big house, because I travelled in my grandfather's Rolls-Royce, then because I sailed through exams and did well at sport. I worked hard—it wasn't sheer luck. Paul's big weakness is that he expects things to happen to him, instead of his going out to look for it. I fail to see why he should mind me being a trustee. He never did get on with your aunt, as you know. I can remember her calling him cheeky—one of the things she hated most.'

'Of course you were never cheeky,' Cilla said angrily. 'Why do you always pick on poor Paul? We're not all made the same.'

'I forgot you're another of his fans,' said Theo, his voice scornful. 'He can do no wrong.'

'No, it isn't that.' Cilla was angry. 'It's just that you're so unfair to him. You take it for granted that whatever he does he shouldn't do, yet how are you to know his side of it?'

'Look, I asked you a simple question. Can I

57

have a straightforward answer? I asked you why Joanna doesn't want Paul to know I'm one of the trustees.'

'I told you—because he's jealous of you . . . it isn't only your money, it's . . . it's . . .' Cilla hesitated, but she was so annoyed she went on. 'He's jealous because of Joanna.'

'Joanna?' Theo laughed, shaking his head. 'He must be out of his mind! I've known your sister for years. No, that's absurd. She must have some other idea in her clever little mind.'

Yes, she has, Cilla was thinking. Joanna doesn't want to let Paul know that she's pleased you're one of the trustees, because she thinks she can get what she wants out of you. But can she? Cilla wondered, looking at the stern face of the man opposite her, gazing with that strange narrowing of his eyes as if he was able to see inside her mind.

'That reminds me, Cilla,' Theo went on. 'You were a fool to go for that climb with Paul. It's a dangerous walk, easy to slip or trip over something. You could have had a nasty fall.'

'Paul helped me.'

'Did he now?' There was that strange smile on Theo's face again. 'Has it never struck you that when you die everything could go to Joanna? That would suit Paul nicely.'

'He did ask . . .' Cilla began, and stopped. She jumped up to her feet and glared at Theo. 'Are you suggesting that Paul would . . . would . . .'

58

'Murder you? Goodness, no.' Another of those strange smiles, Cilla thought. 'He wouldn't murder you. But there might be a tragic accident. You, sliding on the slippery rocks—Paul risking his life to save you, but you might have toppled over the side of that fall and that would have been the end of you. Paul would do anything for Joanna.'

Cilla could find no answer, for she could only agree with that last remark. She knew that Paul would do anything for Joanna, anything at all. Cilla shivered as she thought of the moment when she had looked down that narrow ravine at the churning water below. How easy for her to slip . . . to fall.

But she was .sure Paul would never do it. Paul liked her, and she trusted him.

'Was it—pretty bad with Joanna?' Theo was asking. Again his voice had changed. This time it was sympathetic. 'I felt sorry for you when Anthony and I walked off. Unfortunately this was something you had to face. How did she react?' He frowned. 'Please sit down.'

She had no choice so she sat down. 'Joanna was—well, it was pretty unpleasant until . . . until Paul came.'

'He was on your side?'

'He said he believed me and that Aunt Lil had the right to do what she liked.'

'Joanna doesn't believe you?'

'I don't think so.' Cilla began to twist her fingers together. 'I had one very bad moment.

Two neighbours came in to play bridge . . .'

'John and Lucy Grove?'

'Yes. I'd forgotten their name, but I think it was that.'

'Well?'

'Well, it's hard to explain.' Cilla looked up at him. 'It was the way she said something like: "Oh, this is the sister." Maybe I imagined it, but it was just as if she was thinking, "That awful sister who stole poor Joanna's money." I really felt she was thinking that.'

'Unfortunately you're probably right,' Theo told her gravely. 'You know how people hear one thing and twist it. I'm afraid Lucy is that kind. She has nothing to do but chat, and chat she does. Look, Cilla, you know and I know and Paul knows and Joanna knows very well that you're not the kind of girl to do such a thing. Anyone who really knows you must know that. As Peter said, if they're fool enough to believe you could do such a thing, they're not worth knowing.'

'But it hurts,' she sighed.

'I can imagine. I doubt if Aunt Lil realised it. I honestly think she did it because of her love for you and Joanna.'

'Oh yes, so do I,' agreed Cilla. 'She meant well, but . . .'

'Let's hope it'll all work out right. I suppose you told Joanna you would give her as much money as you were allowed to give?'

'Yes, I did. I said I could also give her

60

presents. You couldn't object to that?'

'Of course not. So long as it's not diamonds and mink coats that can be sold,' Theo said, a smile slightly showing as he spoke.

'I thought I'd get a car . . .' Cilla looked at him anxiously. Should she have bought the car first? she wondered. 'One does need a car here,' she added hastily.

He smiled. 'An excellent idea. You, Anthony and I will go into Victoria this afternoon and buy the car. It's something Joanna has wanted for a long time. It will make her very happy.'

'Hi, Uncle!' a young shrill voice called, and Anthony came racing across the lawn. 'He's super, absolutely super!' he said, and smiled at Cilla. 'Hullo,' he said.

'Hullo. Was he a nice horse?'

'It was smashing!' Anthony's young face was radiant with happiness. 'You haven't seen the dogs? They're super, too.'

'Look, Ant, we're going to have lunch in Victoria,' Theo put in. 'I said we'd go there this afternoon, but you're back sooner than I expected.'

Anthony's face clouded. 'Suppose Mum comes?'

'I'll leave a message at the airport and here. It's only a few miles away. Cilla wants to buy a car. I thought you might like to help her choose one.' Theo turned to Cilla. 'You can drive?'

'Of course. I've got my own car in England.

61

Aunt Lil gave it to me.'

'This'll be child's play after driving there. Only thing is there are a lot of cyclists,' he warned.

'I'll go and change,' Anthony said happily. 'I'll be quick.'

'Okay.' They watched him run across the lawn to the house, then Theo turned to Cilla, his face grave. 'I'm sorry for that kid. He's never known what a real home is, or a real parent for that matter. My sister Noreen should never have had a child. She and Mike are those kind of restless people who never settle down. That's why Anthony got himself expelled.'

'Expelled? From school?'

'Where else? Didn't it strike you that it was an odd time for him to be leaving school? The holidays aren't for another month or so. He admitted it to me, rather proudly. He did everything he could think of to get into trouble. In the end he succeeded and got expelled. They wrote to his parents and my sister gave them this address. Actually they should have been here by now.'

'They will come?' Cilla knew a sudden fear. 'Anthony loves his mother so much.'

'I know. It's a funny thing, Cilla, but so often where a mother shows no love for her children, they adore her. I know I did. My parents spent most of their time arguing and fighting, we kids just fitted in where we could.

It sounds daft, I know, but I always hoped that one day she would love me . . . but they were both killed in a car accident, so she never did.'

Puzzled, Cilla stared at him, for this was a side to his character she had never thought of. Now his face was sad as he talked as if he was thinking aloud.

'It's odd, but Anthony reminds me of myself. I was always doing outrageous things in the hope of getting attention. I never succeeded. Anthony is trying the same. He won't succeed either.'

'But all he wants is a home and some horses and dogs . . .' Cilla stopped. She had nearly said 'Just like me', but stopped because she didn't want Theo to sneer at her 'dreams'.

'I know. This is where I want your help,' Theo went on.

'My help?' Cilla began, and again stopped, remembering that at Joanna's, Theo had said that. 'What can I do?'

'It's like this. I'll stay here as long as I can, but I've an important meeting in South America I must go to and I can't just leave Anthony on his own. I'd ask Joanna, but I know she hates kids.'

'She never did like them.'

'And you? You needn't tell me.' Theo was smiling at her. 'According to Anthony you're super. You really made that long flight pleasant for him.'

'He did for me. He's very bright . . .'

'Like his uncle!' Theo said with a laugh. 'I wondered if you'd move into my house while I'm away and look after the boy? You can go riding. I've got a good groom and staff.'

'I'm coming, I'm coming!' Anthony chanted as he raced towards them, his eyes shining happily.

'Will you?' Theo asked quietly.

She looked at him. 'Need you ask?' she said.

CHAPTER SEVEN

Theo proved to be an intensely interesting courier, Cilla thought, as she sat silently in the back of the long green car with Theo and Anthony while the chauffeur drove.

'The Seychelles,' Theo said, 'are a *confetti*— as the travel brochures call it—of islands. We're a thousand miles off the East African coast. The islands were first colonised by the French and then in 1794 by the English. Actually, Ant, there are no indigenous people here. Know what that word means?'

'Of course I do. *Indigenous* means something that was born there—like plants that weren't brought in from another country.'

Theo laughed. 'Good for you! Same applies here. No one lived here, as far as we know, before the middle of the eighteenth century. When the French came they brought their slaves—so did the British, I'm sorry to say. Then the Indian and Chinese traders came in and they all intermarried, and you'll see from the results that they're a real mix-up.'

'Aren't they called Creoles?' asked Anthony. 'When I knew Mum and Dad were coming here, I got a book from the library about it.'

'Yes. Good for you, Ant. You probably know more than I do about it,' Theo said, laughing.

'Go on, Uncle.'

Theo looked at Cilla. 'Not bored?'

'Far from it,' she said. 'I think it's all too beautiful for words. Those little coves with the white sand and those huge waves . . .'

'That reminds me, both of you. If you go exploring the rocks with their bright-coloured little fish and tiny crabs, do remember to wear rope-soled shoes. We'll get two pairs today. I'm dead serious, you must be careful walking over the rocks, because you can be bitten, with dangerous results. I'm not joking,' he added seriously. 'In addition, you must only swim in the lagoons and then watch out. In the deep water there are hundreds of sharks. You'll probably see some dolphins, too, having a game.'

'Dolphins are great—so clever,' said Anthony. 'Mum took me to a show in London and the dolphins were smashing.'

Cilla was listening, but she was also looking with wonder at the lovely colours: a tall bush of pink camellias, and the large purple flowers. Then there were the flamboyants with their scarlet flowers as well as the wonderful little birds of every colour imaginable. Some little birds kept swooping down and were gone before you had time to look at them.

'One thing—there are no crocodiles here,' Theo was saying. 'Snakes, yes, and lizards and tortoises, of course. We must get hold of a schooner and go to the other islands. Some of them are fantastic. There's Frigate Island where you can see one of the world's most rare birds, the magpie robin. Then there's Praslin which is supposed by some to be the original Garden of Eden, and Cousin Island is another fascinating place. Tens of thousands of birds live on the island, no human beings. And a colony of giant tortoises, many several hundred years old.'

'Whew!' Anthony whistled softly. 'Uncle, would you buy me a camera? I'd love to take photos of them all.'

'Sure, Ant.'

'How big is this island, Uncle?'

Anthony was really enjoying himself, Cilla thought. What a strange man Theo was. A real Jekyll and Hyde. He could be so unpleasant, so brief and curt, even sarcastic, and then in a moment he could be this sympathetic, pleasant man, making sure his insecure, unhappy nephew was given a good time.

'About seventeen miles long and about five miles broad,' he told the boy.

'Is that all?' Anthony was surprised. 'And that?' He looked up at the mountain that stood gaunt, and yet beautiful, covered as it was by the palm trees.

'Morne Seychelles is three thousand feet high.'

'What do they grow for a living, Uncle?'

'Copra . . . from the coconuts. That's why there's always the sweet sickly smell.'

'I like it,' said Cilla.

Theo gave her a strange look. 'You would,' he said curtly, and turned back to Anthony. 'Just think of how old this place is, Ant. Many of these waterfalls have been here for a thousand million years.'

Anthony whistled softly. 'It makes you think!'

Victoria proved to be a busy town, the streets full of people who were, as Theo had said, of many different kinds. Most of the shops were serviced with amazing politeness by Indians in white suits, or Chinese. With Theo's help, Cilla bought several thin dresses and Anthony some thin cotton shorts and shirts, as well as a camera. Anthony was obviously having the time of his life. He couldn't stop talking or asking questions. This gave Cilla time to stand quietly back and study Theo.

He fascinated her. True, he irritated and annoyed her, especially when he said such nasty things about poor Paul, yet at the same time this unexpectedly tender, fatherly way he was treating Anthony was amazing. Somehow it didn't go with the brusque, efficient, impatient, arrogant air Theo normally had.

The car was a sports car, bright red. Cilla fell in love with it at sight and so did Anthony. Theo made Cilla sit in the driver's seat and drive him a short distance. Then he nodded.

'You're okay. Have it if you want it.'

'Of course I do,' said Cilla. The hard part was going to be letting Joanna think the car was hers! It must be Cilla's while she was on the island, she decided.

How long would she be here? She turned to ask Theo, but he and Anthony had plunged into one of the stores.

Cilla waited for them, looking round. There was a ship in the harbour, anchored by one of the jetties. Along the shore she could see glimpses of white buildings seeming to look shyly through the screens of trees. There were huge rocks suddenly appearing unexpectedly next door to modern buildings. There was a cathedral and a statue of Queen Victoria. Cilla found the narrow winding streets fascinating to look at, particularly because the balconies of the old wooden houses seemed to bump into one another across the roads.

The people all seemed to be so happy, jostling one another, walking in the middle of the road, laughing and talking.

Cilla wandered back towards the garage where the car awaited her. No sign of Theo or Anthony? No sign either of the long green car. Had Theo gone home, leaving her to drive her new car? she wondered. The garage proprietor came out and handed her the car keys with a courteous bow. She would be happy, he said he hoped, and that the car was beautiful, as beautiful as its new mistress.

Slightly embarrassed, Cilla got in the car

and drove slowly towards the main road that led along the coast. Theo was right, she thought; there mightn't be the traffic of England, but there were hundreds of bicycles and rickshaws and everyone seemed to view the roads as belonging to them. She drove slowly, sounding her horn and being given startled, rather shocked glances as if she was committing an offence in telling them to get out of the way, but at last she got out on to the road. She still drove slowly though the car went like a bird. She found herself singing. She was happy—so very happy, she thought. This was the loveliest place in the world. Not even in the wildest of her dreams had she imagined anything as beautiful as this.

It was only as she drove into Joanna's drive that Cilla remembered Theo had said they would have lunch in Victoria!

Had it been an invitation or an order? she wondered. Well, he and Anthony and the green car had all vanished, so it had been natural enough for her to feel dismissed.

Joanna came out into the garden, yawning, rubbing her eyes.

'What on earth . . .' she began, frowning.

Cilla got out of the car. 'Ours,' she smiled. Isn't she beautiful?'

'I don't think so,' said Joanna petulantly. 'A sports car!' Her voice was scornful. 'Grow up, Cilla. What we could do with is a big posh-looking car.'

'I like this,' said Cilla, surprised and rather hurt by Joanna's reaction.

'I thought you bought it for me,' Joanna said accusingly.

'I did,' Cilla said, her temper growing. 'You can sell it when I go.'

'When will that be?' Joanna asked.

Cilla couldn't speak for a moment. 'As soon as I'm allowed,' she said, and got into the car, ignoring Joanna who was shouting.

As she drove away, Cilla scolded herself for losing her temper. If she had bought a Rolls-Royce it wouldn't have satisfied Joanna, for nothing could ever satisfy her, she should have known that. Poor Paul, Cilla thought, and realised suddenly that she was automatically driving back to Victoria. Maybe because having lunch with Theo and Anthony was far more enjoyable than staying with Joanna when she was in one of her moods.

Carefully parking the car, Cilla began her search for the green car, glancing also in the shops to see if she could find Theo and Anthony. It was difficult in the crowded streets, looking in every store, searching the car parks. Finally she decided they must have driven back to Theo's home as she had thought in the beginning. He had helped her shop, shown her the island and got her the car she wanted. Why should he bother any more? As she was surprisingly hungry, she hunted for the sort of restaurant she would like.

She was about to cross the road when she heard a voice shouting

'Cilla . . . Cilla! Here she is, Uncle!'

It was Anthony, racing towards her, grabbing hold of her.

'We lost you,' he said accusingly. 'You frightened us.'

Theo was close behind him. His face pale, his mouth stern.

'Where the hell have you been?' he asked. 'We've gone nearly mad looking for you. I rang up your sister's and she said you were in a temper and had driven off somewhere.'

'I couldn't find you either,' said Cilla. 'I hunted everywhere and even the car had gone. So . . . so I thought you'd taken Anthony home and . . . and took it for granted I'd drive myself in the new car.'

'Hadn't I said we'd have lunch here?' Theo demanded.

'Yes, but I didn't remember that until I was at Joanna's.'

'Why were you angry with her?'

'That's my . . .' she began, and then shrugged; he probably wouldn't believe her, because he obviously thought Joanna was wonderful! 'I was upset,' Cilla confessed. 'I thought the car was marvellous, but Joanna didn't. She wanted a posh Rolls-Royce.'

Theo laughed. 'She was joking. You do swallow the bait, Cilla. Come along, let's go and eat. Anthony and I are starving.'

72

'So am I,' Cilla said.

Anthony shook his head. 'Don't ever do that to us again, Cilla,' he said with a pompous solemnity that reminded her of Theo in one of his moods. 'We were worried stiff, weren't we, Uncle?'

Theo laughed. 'We certainly were. Ah, just across the road here. Pleasant place and good food.'

The restaurant was surprisingly crowded, mostly with English or Americans. Theo led the way when the head waiter came hurrying, almost falling over in his eagerness, and bowing politely at Cilla.

'Yes, *monsieur*, the table, it is prepared. This way, if you would be so kind,' he said.

Their progress was slow, for Theo kept stopping at different tables, greeting the people sitting there, introducing Cilla as his friend and Anthony as his nephew. She was greeted with smiles and curious eyes and she wondered if many of them were thinking she might be Theo's fiancée. That made her want to laugh, it was such a crazy idea. Theo had his own interests and marriage was certainly not one of them.

The lunch was excellent, with Anthony thoroughly enjoying himself, Theo and Cilla chatting impersonally.

'If we may, Anthony and I are coming home with you,' Theo said after he had paid and they walked out into the hot sunshine. 'I've sent the car home.'

Cilla had to laugh. 'That gives me no choice, then.'

Theo smiled. 'Exactly. By the way, you'll be getting invitations from some of those people you met today. If you're asked to an evening party or dinner, let me know and I'll take you.'

Startled, Cilla stared at him. 'But why should you? I mean, it's very kind,' she added hastily, 'but I don't want to be a nuisance.'

'You won't be. I don't allow people to be nuisances,' Theo said with his bland arrogance. 'Don't forget I'm your trustee and Aunt Lil made me promise to look after you. I'm not one to break my word.'

'It's . . . it's very good of you,' said Cilla. 'Was that why you introduced me to so many people?'

'Yes, I want everyone to know that I believe you, that I know you're not the sort of monster the grapevine will make you if given a chance.'

Which was very good of him, Cilla thought as they went to her new car, but it meant she was under a . . . well, a sort of obligation to him for being so good, and the odd thing was that she didn't want to have to feel grateful to him for anything!

Driving the car, at first she felt nervous and ill at ease, wondering if Theo would criticise her and become a back-seat driver. But, as she soon found, she need not have worried, since Theo took not the slightest notice or showed

74

any interest whatsoever in her driving. He talked all the time to Anthony, pointing out the birds, giving them their names, telling him about the coconut palms that could live for seventy to a hundred years, how they had nuts all the year round and could also grow as tall as eighty feet. He also promised to show Anthony how to tap two sticks together with which they would call a little bird called 'the flightless rail'. They both laughed and Cilla felt the odd one out, as she drove carefully, her eyes watchful, for she didn't want to do anything wrong.

When they reached Theo's house, Anthony looked at Cilla and then at his uncle.

'Can I show her the horses and dogs?' he asked eagerly.

Theo ruffled the boy's hair. 'Not now, son. You run round and give Pierre a helping hand. I want to talk to Cilla. By the way, ask Ermyntrude to bring us out some coffee. I fancy some.' As Anthony raced towards the house, Theo looked at Cilla. 'Well?' he asked.

Somehow she knew what he meant. 'He's a different child,' she said slowly. 'Honestly, Theo, you are making him happy.'

'Let's sit down. I'm enjoying it, too. I only wish I hadn't got to leave him.'

'You still haven't heard from your sister?' Cilla asked as they walked across the lawn. She kept turning her head, drinking in the beauty of it all. What made the colours so vivid? The

75

reds—the blues—the dramatic purples—the pure white—the lovely warm golden?

'Your neck stiff?' Theo asked as they sat down.

'My neck?' Cilla was startled. 'No. Why?'

'You keep turning your head from side to side.'

She had to laugh. 'I was just looking at everything. It's all so beautiful. You know, Theo, I just can't understand why Joanna never told us how beautiful it was.'

'You find it beautiful?'

'Do I find it beautiful?' Cilla echoed. 'It's . . . too lovely for words. I just wish Aunt Lil could have seen it.'

'You could have both come out to visit Joanna.'

'We were never asked.' Cilla rubbed the edge of the deck chair. 'Maybe we should have suggested it, but Aunt Lil was . . .'

'Proud and hurt by your sister's behaviour. I take it Aunt Lil never tried to stop the marriage?'

'No, she never tried, but there was a feeling. You know the kind? A sort of disappointment. Paul says that Aunt Lil hated him because his father jilted her.'

'His father jilted Aunt Lil? With all that wealth. A likely story,' Theo said contemptuously. 'More likely Aunt Lil discovered the kind of man Paul's father was and jilted him. Paul thinks up some funny

76

stories.'

'His mother told him.'

'Do you honestly think your Aunt Lil would bear malice all those years? Do you believe she would allow herself?'

'No, I don't. I was surprised,' Cilla confessed.

'I'm surprised you even believed it for a moment. I thought you knew Aunt Lil better than that. Paul just making up something to make him seem the victim . . .

A tall Creole girl with beautiful features and long black hair brought out a tray with the coffee.

'Thanks, Ermyntrude,' he said. 'Like to play mother, Cilla? I like mine black, please, and four lumps of sugar.'

'Ermyntrude . . . what a strange name,' she commented.

'You'll come across some odd names here. I think it dates back to the days when the slaves' children were given their master's name or that of one of his family—Hildegarde, Josephine, Carmelite. Sometimes it's the name of a saint, that usually comes when they live near a Mission.'

'Are there schools and hospitals here?'

'Of course there are. This is a sophisticated, civilised place. Unfortunately for us—though fortunately for the locals—more and more tourists and retired people are coming here, to visit or even live.'

'Like you.'

He smiled. *'Touché!* Yes, I know it's a good thing for the islands, but it is rather spoiling things.'

'Progress always does,' she sighed.

'I often wonder what is progress,' Theo mused.

Maybe these locals were happier before the tourists came. Maybe they weren't.'

'Hi, Uncle!' Anthony came running. He seemed so full of life that he couldn't waste time by walking, Cilla thought. How lovely for him if his parents liked the island and decided to settle here. If they decided to settle down anywhere, that was the problem, Cilla realised. 'You know that stallion, Kamasta? Well, he's sort of limping. I wish you'd come and see. Pierre says it's nothing, but . . .'

'We'll have a look.' Theo stood up, smiling at Cilla. 'Well, Cilla, it's been a pleasant day but hot for you, so I expect you're eager to get back to Joanna's and have a bath. We'll be seeing you,' he said. 'Goodbye.'

Feeling as if the chair had been taken away from under her and she tipped out, Cilla stood up quickly. 'Goodbye.'

Anthony grinned. ' 'Bye. See you? You'll come riding?'

'I'd love to.'

'She will,' Theo said curtly. 'Let's get going.' He strode away across the lawn, Anthony close behind.

Cilla finished her cup of coffee as she stood

78

up. Well, Theo could not make it more plain if he spelled out the words. She was merely a responsibility—he would keep his word to Aunt Lil and look after her 'young niece'. Also, Cilla realised, he was going to make use of her where his nephew was concerned. Otherwise she was a nothing. She might just as well be a robot, something so impersonal that you didn't know it was there.

She walked to her car, wishing she could see the inside of the house, or the dogs and horses. Why had Theo stopped her from seeing them? One thing, when she was living there with Anthony, she would be able to explore, so she must just be patient and wait.

CHAPTER EIGHT

The next few weeks passed quickly, with Theo taking Anthony and Cilla out every day as he had promised, to the different islands where Anthony used his new camera, his young face so happy that it made Cilla want to cry. Anthony was really enjoying every moment. He had even got an exercise book in which he carefully wrote down notes.

'So I can tell Mum,' he explained gravely to Cilla one day. 'She'll be interested,' he added as he gave her the book to read.

I do hope so, Cilla thought as she read the notes.

'We saw a weaver bird, it's called *toc-toc*, but I don't know why. We also saw a chameleon. It has funny long legs, walks slowly, and if it is frightened, it stands still, twisting itself so that it looks just like a leaf. We also saw kestrels. They eat dead lizards. I like lizards, they move so fast. We saw lots of spiders. They are huge but don't hurt you. The white terns make strange screeching noises. We also saw giant tortoises, two hundred years old.'

'I think Ant would make a good ornithologist,' was Theo's comment.

'What's an ornithologist?' Anthony asked. Cilla had to admit that she didn't know either.

Theo laughed. 'Someone who studies birds

and their habits. You have to go to college to study, of course, but then you can travel anywhere in the world.'

'Sounds good, but . . .' Anthony paused, obviously uncertain. Cilla smiled at him sympathetically, for she knew he longed for a permanent home—one where he could have a horse and dogs.

It was strange, but Cilla saw little of Paul these days; he brought home work with him and immediately after their dinner would vanish into his study. Not that it made Joanna any more friendly, as it was obvious she was annoyed because Cilla was going out every day with Theo and Anthony. Not that she said anything, but there was a silent sort of atmosphere in the house which Cilla hated. It grew worse when the invitations out to dinner or to parties came in for Cilla, who was always escorted by Theo.

'Why is Theo taking you out all the time?' Joanna asked once after he had phoned. 'Are you having an affair?'

Cilla had to laugh. 'An affair? Why, we fight most of the time. He's only doing this because he promised Aunt Lil he would look after me.'

Joanna laughed scornfully. 'As if you need looking after! You're with me and . . . well, I can't see why he need take you everywhere. Are you sure he isn't in love with you?'

Again Cilla had to laugh. 'We're always arguing or fighting. He's just doing his duty.

He's taking me out on purpose.'

'On purpose?' Joanna, beautiful as usual, looked sceptical. 'For what purpose?'

Cilla hesitated and then decided to tell the truth. 'Because he wants to stop the talk about me on the island.'

'What talk?' Joanna asked, but Cilla saw the red flush that slid over her sister's face. 'You know very well what I mean,' she snapped, suddenly angry, for Joanna's behaviour hadn't helped at all. Cilla mimicked an affected voice and said: 'Is this the cruel, selfish sister who stole all the money from poor Joanna?'

Joanna's cheeks were bright red and she fidgeted as she lay on the swing chair in her yellow kaftan. 'That's absurd. No one says that.'

'Don't they?' Cilla laughed bitterly. 'They may not always say it in those words, but they imply it.'

'That's ridiculous! You're making it up.'

'I am not!' Cilla's voice was angry. 'Theo knows that, too, and that's why he takes me out and introduces me to people—to show them that he doesn't believe I'm that sort of girl, who would make Aunt Lil forget you were her niece. If anyone did that, Joanna,' she finished, standing up, 'it was you. You never wrote to Aunt Lil. She used to worry about you. You believe I did it deliberately, don't you? That's why I hate living here with you. I know you and Paul don't want me . . .'

Joanna sat up quickly. 'That's absurd. We like to have you with us. I'm sure you're imagining it all, Cilla. I can't think anyone would believe you did it on purpose.'

Cilla hesitated. Should she believe that, or was Joanna only saying it because she wanted to get as much money as she could out of her sister? It was a horrible thought, but, knowing Joanna, she could not help thinking it was true. 'I'm not imagining it, Joanna. Only last night at the Beavers' party a woman said to me: "I think your sister is a wonderful woman, to be so nice to you."' Cilla gave a bitter little laugh and turned to hurry to the house; she had to shower and change as Theo was calling for her within an hour.

The bitterness stayed with her the whole evening and as Theo drove her home, he glanced at her.

'What are you mad about?' he asked.

His arrogant sarcastic voice was amused, which annoyed her still more.

'I am not mad,' she said coldly.

Theo drove the car off the main road, parking it on a stretch of grass, and then he turned round to look at her.

'Yes, you are,' he said curtly, 'so don't lie. What's wrong? Have you and Joanna had a row? Or are you getting bored because you've been out with me and Anthony so much?'

She was startled and turned impulsively. 'Of course not! I've enjoyed it all and so has

Anthony. Very much indeed.'

'Then if it isn't that, what is it?' he asked, the moon shining on his face, his voice impatient.

She knew Theo well enough to know that he would give her no peace until he got the truth out of her so she told him. She twisted her hands together, looking at them as she said: 'It's just that . . . that I can't stand much more. They all believe I got Aunt Lil's money and that I'm a horrible selfish person and Joanna is a wonderful martyr for putting up with me, and . . .' She stopped, her voice going husky as she fought the tears which had alarmingly come close.

'Don't be absurd,' Theo said scornfully. 'People don't think that.'

She turned to look at him. 'It's easy enough for you. You're not going through it. If you knew the sort of hints they drop, the things they say.' She quoted several remarks and saw him frown.

'Don't be childish,' he said crossly. 'You're an absolute egoist, Cilla. You should be ashamed of yourself.'

'Egoist? Me?' She nearly choked.

'An egoist,' he said icily, 'is one who values other people's opinions of himself far more than his own knowledge of himself. You know very well why your Aunt Lil left the money as she did. It had little to do with you—she wanted to protect Joanna as well as yourself because she was afraid Paul would gamble away the lot. If she had left it all to you, unconditionally, I wouldn't have been surprised, because Joanna has never been a good niece. Now stop worrying what those gossip-minded people say. I don't believe it, and . . .'

'You've been very good to me,' the words tumbled out of her mouth,' taking me out like this, showing people you don't believe I did it . . .' She stopped abruptly, as his hand shot out and closed round her wrist like an iron bracelet.

'What did you say?' he asked coldly.

'That I'm most grateful to you for coming to take me out so that people will know you didn't believe the gossip and . . .'

'Wait a moment. Let's get this straight. You think I'm taking you out to clear your name?'

'Well, you are, aren't you?' Cilla's eyes were wide and innocent. 'I mean, I do appreciate it, Theo. You've been most kind, but . . .'

'You'd rather I didn't?' he asked sarcastically. She went bright red. 'No, I didn't mean that. I have enjoyed myself very much, but . . . but I didn't want to become a . . . a burden to you and . . .'

'I see.' He gave what sounded like a sigh and switched on the engine. 'So what do you want to do?'

'I'd like to go away—far away.'

He looked at her. 'You can't, you know that

85

very well. Besides, it would look as if you were admitting your guilt. In any case, have you forgotten that you've promised to look after Anthony for me when I'm away? I was counting on you.'

'I know. Of course I'll look after him,' Cilla said quickly, but as so often happened, she realised that she would never understand the man sitting by her side.

He was not the slightest bit concerned or interested in her misery. That didn't matter. He was such a strange man—when they were dancing or at parties, he was charming, and often she felt that he really enjoyed being with her—and then, when they were alone, they were arguing about something or other or else he was asking her to do something for him. That was all she was to him a useful acquaintance. Certainly not a friend.

It was two days before she heard from Theo again. An invitation had come for them, but she had made an excuse as she had known she could not ring up Theo and ask him if he would take her after the unkind words he had said. *Egoist!* Of all things to call her. If only she wasn't always so clumsy with words when talking to Theo, she thought, so slow in thinking.

She was alone having breakfast when he phoned. As she heard the deep vibrant voice, she grew tense, preparing herself for one of their usual arguments. But he was curt, giving her no time to think.

'Sorry at such short notice, Cilla,' he said. 'I have to be off to South America today. I'll send Anthony over to fetch you.'

'How long will you be away?' Cilla asked breathlessly, for she could hear the impatience in his voice.

'I haven't a clue. I should think his parents will have turned up before I get back.'

It was then that Cilla remembered the question she always meant to ask but somehow always forgot to until it was too late. 'Theo . . . Theo,' she said urgently, 'I keep meaning to ask you. How long have I got to stay on the Island? I mean because of the conditions?'

He was not even listening. There was a little click showing he had slammed down the receiver impatiently. He was not concerned with her happiness, only with his interests, she thought bitterly. Surely he could have spared the time to answer? Probably he hadn't even heard the question, as the only person he could think of was himself.

'What's that?' Joanna came along the corridor in her dressing-gown, yawning, brushing back her beautiful red hair. 'Theo—at this hour? He knows I never get up before twelve.'

'It wasn't for you. He's going to South America and I'm moving into his house to look after Anthony.'

'You're—*what*?' Joanna almost shouted.

'Look, you can't do that sort of thing. People will talk.'

'They're talking now,' Cilla shrugged. 'Besides, Theo won't be there, so there won't be anything to talk about.'

'Anthony could have come here. Why didn't Theo think of that? We've known him so long . . .'

'Perhaps that's why. He said you told him you hated children. Look. I must pack. I don't know when the car is coming for me.'

'You're not taking *your* car?' demanded Joanna, giving a little emphasis to the word *your*. Although at the beginning she had said she hated the car, she was always using it when she could.

'Apparently not. What His Majesty says goes.'

'His Majesty?' Joanna was puzzled.

Cilla laughed and walked by her. 'Isn't that what Theo thinks he is? Someone very important, very special, very selfish indeed.'

She hurried down the corridor, not noticing the puzzled look in Joanna's eyes, not realising what her angry words might have betrayed.

Cilla was ready and waiting when the car arrived. Anthony was in it and jumped out of the car as soon as it stopped.

'Can I see the dogs?' he asked.

Cilla looked at Joanna, for when Paul was away, the dogs were generally in their kennels.

'If you like,' Joanna said curtly, picking up a

88

book but only pretending to read it, Cilla noticed, as it was upside down.

Now why was Joanna like that? Cilla could only think she was jealous about everything to do with Theo. Joanna had thought they were such close friends, and now she must be wondering if she had imagined it all.

Walking round the back to the two big kennels and the large yard where the Afghan hounds were, Anthony told her about seeing Uncle Theo off in the plane.

'I hoped Mum might arrive, but the plane is late, so maybe when we get home . . . Oh, aren't they great!' he exclaimed, his voice awed as he saw the dogs.

They were indeed very beautiful—such elegant limbs, lovely faces, silky hair. 'Do you take them for walks?' Anthony asked.

'Paul does, mostly,' Cilla told him.

'Who's Paul?'

'My brother-in-law. My sister's husband.'

'It must be fun having a sister. I wish I had, then we'd have a proper home.'

'Maybe you will one day. Have a brother, I mean,' Cilla told him, and then wondered if she should have said that, for Anthony would be hoping he could have a brother and perhaps be disappointed.

They drove to Cilla's temporary home, Seaview, as Theo had called it. She hardly noticed the beautiful scenery or heard Anthony's chatter; she was thinking of Theo.

How strange and selfish he was! Never once had he invited her into his house. Always they had sat in the garden as if he was determined not to let her become involved in his life-as if she must be kept as an outsider, an unfortunate and irritating burden he had been given by Aunt Lil.

Anthony showed her the house proudly, saying Theo was one of the finest architects in the world. It was a beautiful house, there was no doubt, Cilla thought, as she was shown round. There was a simplicity about it that made it so different from Joanna's house which, until that moment, Cilla had thought was the most beautiful she had seen.

'Like it?' Anthony asked, smiling up at her as he took her in the rooms with their long glass walls that showed the garden full of flowers, the palm trees that clustered round the mountain and climbed up the steep slopes as if fighting one another for room or the blue sea pounding on the rocks. The house was lovely with the shining polished floors, the dark rugs, the silk curtains. But of the whole building Anthony was most proud of Theo's studio. Anthony led her round the sloping desks, explaining the drawings as Theo had done.

'Uncle Theo is a clever man,' Anthony said proudly.

And a very selfish one; he could be cruel and thoughtless, too, Cilla was thinking, but she didn't want to hurt Anthony.

'What's he working on now, Anthony?' she asked.

'A village in South America. They had a terrible time when there was an earthquake and Uncle Theo is trying to rebuild it and making it look as it was, yet being modern. You know what I mean? Uncle Theo says it's hard for them to realise what a proper bath is, or an indoor loo. He believes old people and young must be gradually taught to accept new ideas.'

Cilla shook her head. She could not understand Theo. He could be so thoughtless of her, yet concerned with the peasants of a South American village.

'Would you like to see Uncle Theo's therapy?' Anthony asked. 'You do know what therapy is? Uncle Theo says he gets fed up with the world and the petty obstacles to his work, so he does this to enjoy himself. I'm allowed to touch these paintings,' he added hastily. He pulled out a number of canvases. 'He's a real artist.'

Cilla agreed as she looked at the paintings—somehow they were so different from what she would have expected from the strong-willed, arrogant, impatient man, for the paintings were peaceful—serene, beautiful, amazingly unlike Theo.

'This is good of me,' Anthony said, producing a painting of a hillside with the dogs chasing the horses and Anthony waving as he rode away.

'It is good,' Cilla agreed. Theo was a man of many talents, she thought. Who would ever have thought he was an artist, too?

He hasn't finished yours yet,' Anthony went on.

'Mine?' Cilla was really startled. Surely Theo wouldn't paint her? Now if it had been her sister with her red hair and lovely skin, Cilla could have understood. But not herself.

Anthony led her to an easel. 'Come round,' he invited.

She followed him, wondering what sort of painting Theo would have done. She stood and stared and it was as if a cold finger slid down her spine.

Was that how he saw her? That girl with the young eager face and long dark hair waving in the breeze that was tossing the palm trees round her? How young she looked! How absurdly young with that pointed rock towering above her, making her look even younger than she was.

'It's good, isn't it?' Anthony said proudly.

'But I look so young!' Cilla could not keep the dismay out of her voice.

'That's your charm,' said Anthony.

'My charm?'

'Uncle Theo says so. I asked him 'cos I like you. You don't talk to me as if I was a schoolboy. You're only ten years older than

92

me. Uncle Theo is much older than you. You don't want to marry a man that old, so why not marry me one day?'

Cilla smiled. 'Thanks for the compliment, but I'm not sure I want to marry,' she said, and knew that it wasn't the truth, for already she had realised how miserable life alone could be. But it would have to be the right man.

'Uncle Theo isn't keen to marry—he says he travels so much he doesn't think any wife would stand it.'

'She would if she loved him.'

Anthony frowned. 'What is *love*, Cilla? They lecture you at school about sex, but no one ever explains what love is.' He sighed. 'I looked it up in the dictionary and it said liking someone.'

'It's more than liking . . .' Cilla said slowly, looking at the painting of herself. 'I've never been in love, so I don't really know, but I think it's when you hate to be away from that person, when you want him to be happy, when you're only really happy when you're with him.'

Anthony led the way to the door. 'That's funny, Cilla, because that's exactly what Uncle Theo said when I asked him.'

'He did?' Cilla was really startled. Somehow she wouldn't have expected Theo to explain what the word meant, and she most certainly would not have expected him to say the same as herself.

'Yes. Look, here are the bedrooms. This is Uncle's.' It was a bedroom with an open door to a bathroom, a wall of glass showing the garden and ocean. There was an austere simplicity about it. The walls were white, so were the curtains and rugs.

'This is mine,' Anthony said as they walked on. 'We've all got our own bathrooms. It's a good idea.' Cilla had a glimpse of a similar room next door. This time the colour was palest yellow.

Hers was the next. Obviously a guest room, it was more elaborate, with wallpaper on the walls, a mixture of gold and apricot colours, with matching curtains and pink rugs.

Her suitcase was on a small table. 'Maybe I should unpack,' she said.

Anthony nodded, looking at his wrist watch. 'You've got twenty minutes. I'll go and talk to the dogs. I thought we'd go for a ride later— it's too hot midday,' he explained. ' 'Bye.'

'Goodbye,' said Cilla.

After the door had slid to, she went to stand by the window. The view was incredibly lovely. No matter how long you stared at it, the more beautiful it became. The colour—the deep green of the grass, the white beach, the palm trees, many of them bent over as the strong winds had forced them to do. It was the most beautiful house she had ever seen, or even dreamed of. A house designed, built and lived in by a bachelor—by a man who was a mixture of different good qualities and irritating bad ones. Why, she wondered, as she unpacked her clothes, was it that every time she and Theo were alone together, they began to argue or to snap at one another? Why was Theo so different at times? Which was the real Theo? she wondered. If only she knew!

CHAPTER NINE

Six weeks were to pass before Cilla was to see Theo again. Not that she would have minded had she been told, for she was still angry with him. Angry because he had made it so plain that he didn't want to get involved in any way with her, so he had never asked her into his house—angry also because when she had thanked him gratefully for going out of his way to help her, he had immediately turned and scolded her for being an egoist.

That word she could not forget, and it hurt—hurt almost as much as the absurdly young face he had painted of her. Often she stood before a mirror, gazing anxiously at herself. Did she really look so absurdly young? she would ask herself worriedly.

The six weeks flew by, for so much happened. She enjoyed her outings with Anthony, but even more enjoyed going home in the cool of the end of the day to Theo's house. Although Theo was not there every room seemed to whisper a memory of the man who, when actually in flesh and blood facing her, made her so angry and confused. If only she could forget him, she would think. But how could she when every brick of the house made her think of him?

Life with Anthony had been so pleasant and

different from life with Joanna and Paul, where there had always been that icy silence that had upset Cilla and the lonely walks. Suddenly out of the blue and without warning had come Anthony's mother. Never, Cilla often thought as she remembered that day, would she ever forget the joy on Anthony's face as he raced across the lawn to fling himself at his mother.

They had gone in a few days and Cilla had returned, rather reluctantly, to Joanna's house, only to discover, to her surprise and joy, that Joanna had changed completely. Gone was the silent hostility—now Joanna would go shopping with her, would entertain and make her feel at ease and wanted.

It was at one of their dinner parties that Cilla met Colin Paine. It had been a beautiful night with the moon riding high and the palm trees silhouetted against the night. She had liked him at once, a tall man with short dark hair and a friendly smile. They had sat in the moonlight talking and later danced.

When the guests had gone Joanna had teased her. 'Don't say you've fallen for Colin, because he's broken more hearts than anyone on the island,' she had said, laughing.

There was no question of falling in love with Colin, Cilla thought as the days passed, but she did enjoy going out with him.

One day they planned to meet for lunch in Victoria and Cilla had parked her car and was waiting by the market, crowded as usual with shoppers while the women selling their fruit and vegetables squatted on the ground and laughed and chatted. Colin was a little late, so Cilla looked round her; it was unlike him.

She caught her breath with surprise as she saw the tall girl with fair hair and the image of an international beauty. It was the girl who had seen Cilla and Anthony at the airport and promptly rung up Theo to say his nephew had been kidnapped. What was her name? Fiona Renaud, of course! She had also turned up one day at Theo's house and demanded to know what Cilla was doing there.

Now Cilla gasped, stepping back in the entrance to the restaurant, but it was too late, for it was Theo she had seen, coming out of the shop behind Fiona, and he was staring across the street at Cilla.

Cilla moved fast into the restaurant—she and Colin had been there several times—but Theo moved even faster, crossing the wide street, grabbing her arm.

'What are you doing here?' he asked. 'I told you to look after Anthony, not leave him alone.'

'He's . . .' Cilla began, but Theo was not listening as he hustled her along the street, half carrying her, his voice angry.

'I thought I could trust you to look after the boy!' He jerked open the door of his car and almost threw her in, slamming the door shut, and telling the Creole chauffeur to get going, as he was in a hurry.

Cilla lay back against the seat, completely breathless and so angry she couldn't speak. She closed her eyes.

'Well, haven't you anything to say?' Theo asked angrily.

She drew a deep breath and opened her eyes. 'When you give me the chance,' she told him. 'Of all the disgusting, rude, impossible . . . !' She lost her breath again.

He was smiling. 'I see. I'm the one who's misbehaving, am I? Yet isn't it natural that I'm worried about my nephew? His parents have put him in my care and I ask you to look after him—and then I find you romping around the town, not caring one bit!' Theo's voice had hardened. 'Hadn't you better explain?'

Her breath back again, her anger a little more under control, Cilla smiled triumphantly.

'Your nephew is now in England.'

'He's what?' For once Cilla saw she had won. Theo was looking startled. 'His parents turned up?'

'His mother did. His father is in hospital in England.'

Suddenly Theo was laughing. 'I might have known you weren't the type who'd let me down. I should have known when Fiona said . . .'

'Fiona!' Cilla exclaimed scornfully. 'She came to see you, and did she throw her weight about!'

Theo was laughing. 'I can imagine! What did she want?'

'You. She was furious because you hadn't written to tell her you were going away.'

'She happened to be away herself. Besides, I haven't time to let everyone know my plans.'

'She seemed to think she had a right to know . . .'

Cilla began, then stopped, wondering if it was unfair to Fiona to say that, but Theo merely laughed. 'She has some funny ideas, that girl.'

'She's very lovely,' Cilla pointed out.

'To look at, perhaps.'

'Why don't you paint her?' Cilla asked.

'Oh—so Anthony showed you my paintings, did he?'

'Yes. He's very proud of you.'

'What did you think of them? Did you see the one I'm doing of you?' Cilla hesitated and her face must have betrayed her, for Theo laughed. 'You didn't like it, eh?'

'I look so young,' she complained.

'You are so young.'

'I'm over twenty!'

He laughed again. 'Only just. You've got a long way to go yet. That reminds me—Fiona told me you often went out dancing of an evening with some man.'

'Well, I wouldn't go with some girl, would I?' Cilla snapped.

100

He chuckled and then his voice became different, cold, accusing so she felt her body stiffen as she prepared herself for the row she knew was coming.

'Fiona told me you were going out with Colin Paine.'

'And why shouldn't I?'

'Because he's a real womaniser, a no-good man. Who introduced you?' He snapped his fingers so loudly she jumped. 'I bet it was your brother-in-law.'

'And why not? He's an old friend of theirs.'

'A likely story!' Theo sneered. 'They know that when you're married, you can do what you like with Aunt Lil's money, so they produced Colin. I'm right, aren't I?'

Cilla began to speak and then closed her mouth. She stared at him, trying to find words that would do, but all the time she could not forget what had happened after one of Colin's visits. Joanna had teased her, saying Colin had fought off more predatory females than any man save Theo. Paul had put his arm round Cilla's shoulders and said it was a pity, because marriage had its advantages. Cilla had gone to her bedroom, but found she had left something in the large lounge. As she hurried back to get it she could hear Joanna and Paul talking, and then Paul had said, his voice harsh with anger:

It's got to work. It's our only chance.'

'It'll work,' Joanna had said comfortingly,

101

and Cilla had gone back to her bedroom, wondering what they had been talking about, not wanting them to think she was eavesdropping.

Theo's suggestion now made her look on those words with a different view. Could Theo be right and Joanna and Paul be trying to get her married so that they could get Joanna's share of Aunt Lil's money without any more trouble?

But her loyalty to Paul was stronger than Theo's suggestion.

'You are the end!' she said angrily. 'You're always accusing poor Paul—first of trying to murder me and now to marry me off. There's no question of that. Colin is a friend of mine, but that's all. You can't stop me having friends.'

'Can't I?' Theo's voice was threatening. 'You'd be surprised. I don't like that man, nor does Peter Kent.'

'He knows Colin?'

'I'll say. Now look—tell me more about Anthony. His mother just walked in, did she? How did you like her?'

Cilla felt the stiffness leave her body, for his voice had changed, losing the harsh threatening note she hated.

'She came by taxi, and Anthony just flung himself in her arms. His father isn't well and is in hospital. She found out you were in South America and decided she'd better come out and fetch the boy as she wasn't sure who was looking after him here. I liked her very much . . .' Cilla hesitated, but decided she wouldn't tell him what Anthony's mother had said to her—that marriage was a difficult partnership; when you had a child and husband your loyalties were torn apart. 'You mustn't let either child or husband feel neglected,' she had said. 'My husband, Mike, is so crazy about seeing the world, but now it'll be Anthony's turn, as we're getting a house in Cornwall because Mike must go slowly for a few years. It isn't easy to do the right thing. Marriage isn't always easy.'

'Her husband is ill and they're buying a house in Cornwall,' she told Theo.

'The kid'll enjoy that.'

'Yes. She's promised him a horse and two dogs,' Cilla laughed.

'You must have missed him?' There was that streak of tenderness in Theo's voice that she sometimes heard, and that always puzzled her, for it was so unlike his usual self.

'I did,' she said, and remembered the awful emptiness in her life when she had seen Anthony and his mother go in the plane and out of her life. 'Luckily, Joanna has changed a lot. We're much better friends than we've ever been.'

'That's good,' Theo said, then spoilt it all by saying: 'I wonder why.'

As usual he was being unfair to Joanna and

Paul.

'I was supposed to be having lunch with Colin today,' Cilla said angrily, 'and I parked my car in town—and now you've brought me out here.'

'Is that so?' Theo looked annoyed. 'Why the hell didn't you tell me?'

'You gave me no chance . . .' Cilla began, but he was paying no attention, but leaning forward to speak to the chauffeur, who slowed up the car and turned it at the first opening.

There was a long silence as the car sped along the road. Cilla's anger grew more and more and suddenly boiled over.

'You owe me an apology,' she said. 'Treating me like that! What must Fiona have thought? It'll be all over the island!'

Theo chuckled. 'I bet it is already. What does it matter?'

'I don't mind that, but . . .'

'I owe you an apology?' he said with a smile. 'I agree! I do apologise for thinking, even for one moment, that you would let me down. I apologise. Am I forgiven?'

Cilla stared at him. He had actually apologised! 'Of course,' she gasped.

CHAPTER TEN

Colin was pacing up and down the crowded pavement when they reached the restaurant. Theo had not spoken a word since he had apologised and Cilla had sat rigidly, gazing blindly out of the car window. When she saw Colin she waited, tense, for Theo to make some comment, but oddly enough he said nothing of the sort.

The car stopped. The chauffeur slid out and opened the door. A little uncertain, Cilla looked at Theo. He looked at her, his face blank.

'No doubt I'll see you some time,' he said sarcastically. 'I hope you enjoy your lunch,' he added as she got out of the car and hurried to join Colin.

Cilla did not enjoy her lunch very much because, for the first time since she had met Colin, he was cross.

'Where on earth have you been? I thought you were ill or something, then I saw your car parked. What were you doing with that man?'

She told him, trying, she found, to defend Theo. 'Of course he was worried about his nephew . . .' she finished.

'That's absurd,' Colin complained. 'He must have known you were to be trusted to look after the boy. He was with Fiona?'

'Yes. She happened to be at the airport when he arrived and she asked for a lift into town.' Colin smiled.

'A likely story! Now she'll have to get someone to give her a lift back to the airport so she can pick up her car. I'm surprised Theo Randall would fall for that. You like the man?' he asked abruptly.

Fortunately the waiter had come with the two huge menus for them to study, so Cilla ignored the question. Of course she didn't like Theo, she told herself. He had no manners at all, he just behaved as he wanted to regardless of how he hurt others.

Later, as Colin walked with her to her parked car, he asked another abrupt question.

'Are you scared of Theo Randall? Why do you put up with such behaviour?'

'Because . . .' Cilla began, but stopped in time, for she had nearly said, 'Because Theo is a trustee, and I don't want to annoy him because he might be difficult about letting me have more money so that I can give it to Joanna.' She felt hot all over, for it had been a narrow escape as Joanna wanted no one to know that Theo was a trustee.

A few days later Colin took her to a special cocktail party at the house of one of the top diplomats. She wondered if Theo would be there—if he would make a scene because she was going with Colin. Well, she told herself, she was not going to allow Theo to run her life. It was bad enough as it was, thanks to well-meaning Aunt Lil. Joanna had persuaded her to buy a new dress, and when Colin saw it, he whistled softly.

He had laughed and turned to Joanna. 'Isn't Cilla delicious, delectable and delightful?' he asked.

Joanna laughed. 'You should know,' she said.

Outside in the dark night he helped her into his car and gently took her chin in his hand, bent down and kissed her—a gentle kiss.

Know something?' he said with a sigh as he slid in by her side. 'I have a horrible feeling I'm falling in love with you.' He made it sound so tragic that Cilla had to laugh.

That sounds like an insult,' she teased.

He started the car. 'It wasn't meant as one. The trouble is I'm a loner. I don't want to get married,' he said almost violently.

Cilla laughed. 'That makes two of us.'

'Don't you want to get married?' Driving down the track, the brilliant lights destroying the darkness and making the trees look like crazy dancers with their pointing branches, Colin asked, 'I thought all girls want to get married?'

'This girl doesn't,' Cilla said, and then realised it was not the truth. For she *did* want to marry, but it would have to be the right man. And how did you find that out?

It was a pleasant party with no accusing eyes

or sarcastic remarks. Her new dress of cream silk with beautifully embroidered smocking on the high waistline was admired by many. Cilla found herself dancing with strangers. She kept herself wary, looking round in case Theo was there. If he was, how would he behave? she wondered. Grab her and take her outside to threaten to do something drastic to prevent her from being friends with Colin? Theo had said he could do just that if he wanted to—yet what could he do, after all? She had a perfect right to have Colin for a friend, and she liked him.

The only unpleasant moment of the evening was when she was dancing with Colin and the humid heat made her cheeks run with water, so she hurried to the powder room. She saw to her dismay that Fiona was there, screwing up her face as she adjusted her false eyelashes. She saw Cilla's reflection in the mirror, so she didn't look round but merely spoke.

'I see you're after Colin now. Good luck. You'll need it, because he's hard to get,' Fiona laughed, her face scornful. 'Anyhow, I'm glad you gave up Theo. You'd only get hurt.'

Cilla felt the rush of anger that Fiona always aroused. 'I haven't given Theo up—I don't want . . .' she was saying as the door opened and several guests joined them. Cilla walked to the other mirror in the room and hastily wiped her face. If Fiona was here, then must Theo be here, too? she wondered. Should she ask

Fiona? There was no chance even had she decided to do so, for the room was getting crowded; everyone was feeling the heat.

As Colin drove her home, Cilla asked him if he knew Fiona.

He laughed. 'Who doesn't? Her family have lived on the island for many years. She's got her eye on Theo Randall, you know.'

'I do know. She's always warning me not to try to get him,' Cilla said.

'And are you trying?' Colin asked, a sharp note in his voice.

'Of course not,' Cilla laughed. 'We fight every time we meet.'

'I'm glad to hear it, because most girls couldn't honestly say that. They're after his charm and his money. He's so wealthy it stinks,' Colin said bitterly. 'Not that it's his fault. He inherited most of his money.'

'I hate money,' Cilla exclaimed suddenly. 'It causes so much misery and . . .'

'And happiness! Depends how you use it.'

'You know about . . .?' Cilla said slowly, wondering if he did know, for they had never discussed it.

'You mean about your aunt's will? I guess everyone does. Poor Joanna went nearly mad with disappointment. She was counting on getting her half . . .'

'She will—one day. Do you think I . . . that it was my fault?'

Colin jammed on the brake so suddenly that

she was nearly flung forward. He drove off the road on to the grass verge, stopped the engine, turned to her and took her in his arms.

'Of course not, you little idiot,' he said tenderly. 'You're not that type of person. No one believes it since they've met you.'

How different he was from Theo, Cilla was thinking. Colin held her gently, his arms cradling her, whereas Theo's fingers would be painfully digging into her arm.

'What do you plan to do? I suppose it isn't so much as what *can* you plan to do? I gathered there were some ridiculous conditions?'

'There are. I've got . . .' She stopped just in time from saying *two trustees*. 'A trustee in England, and he . . . well, he . . .'

'Calls the tune?'

'Yes. It's infuriating,' she sighed. 'It must be. What if you marry?'

'I get the money,' she told him.

'All of it?'

She laughed. 'Half of it, because I'll give Joanna her half.'

'I wonder if she'd do the same,' Colin said slowly.

He kissed her lightly. 'I doubt it. You're a very different person from your sister.' Gently he let go of her, pushing her along the seat. 'We'd better get going or I may say something I'll regret.'

'What could that be?' she laughed as he

110

started the car. 'You sound scared.'

'I am—of you,' he told her. 'I'm anti-marriage, you see. I like to be free to roam. Tell me,' he laughed as he spoke, 'do you dig me?'

'I'll dig a hole for you if you don't drive me home. I'm tired,' Cilla said, relieved that they were now joking. She was rather disturbed by what he had said. Marriage was a serious thing. She liked Colin, but was liking enough?

Next day at lunch Joanna said: 'The grapevine says Theo is back.'

'He's been back quite a few days,' Cilla told her, helping herself to a second lot of the delicious crab salad.

'And he's never been to see you? A fine sort of trustee,' Joanna said with a laugh.

Joanna was in one of her good moods, so Cilla felt relaxed and was able to talk.

'We had quite a scene in town . . .' she began, and told Joanna about Theo's anger, his almost forcing her down the street to his car, accusing her of neglecting Anthony, and then his anger because she—according to Fiona—was going out with Colin. Talking so easily made Cilla suddenly worried. Had she said too much or had she stopped in time? She didn't want Joanna to know of the horrible things Theo had said about her and Paul—that they were trying to get Cilla married so that Joanna could get her half of the money!

Cilla was relieved when Joanna laughed. 'I

111

can't understand Theo these days. In the past he often used to drop in and have a drink and chat with me.' She laughed. 'When Paul was at work, of course, because those two just don't get on. Theo is a difficult person.'

'You're telling me,' Cilla agreed. 'At times he's absolutely intolerable!'

'Is he as bad as that?' Joanna asked with a smile. Cilla had to laugh. 'Even worse,' she said.

'That's the understatement of the year.'

'Surely as you're his ward, he ought to keep an eye on you?' said Joanna.

'Oh, he does that all right, but he only gets in touch with me when he wants me to do something for him. And he—yes, *he*—had the nerve to call me an egoist.'

'An egoist?' Joanna was puzzled. 'Now what made him say that?'

Once again Cilla realised she was going too close to things it was better not to talk about as no one lately had suggested she was 'that bad sister who had deliberately cheated Joanna,' so it was best to avoid it and Cilla changed the subject.

'Colin is taking me to a wedding on Sunday,' she said. 'One of the local lads that used to work for him, he said.'

'They can be very colourful, but surely rather a bore when you don't know the bride or groom?'

'Colin said . . .' Cilla began, but stopped in

112

time and altered the sentence. 'It would be a sort of . . . well, something local and therefore interesting. He says it nearly bankrupts the bridegroom, because he has to put on such an expensive show.'

Cilla wondered what Joanna would say if she was told the exact words Colin had used: 'It might make it easier for me if I saw how happy the couple was. Marriage scares me still, Cilla, yet whenever I'm with you . . .' and he had kissed her fingers in turn, half joking yet with a seriousness that impressed her.

*   *   *

She and Colin drove along the coast to Victoria where the town shone in the sunlight and the local men were walking round the market, like peacocks in their bright gaudy shirts. Some had Chinese features, other Indian, even more were a strange mixture of various nationalities. The local girls sauntered by, their heads held high, their hips swinging as they glanced flirtatiously at the men.

'The poor bridegroom pays for the wedding and builds a house too,' Colin was saying. 'It takes him years to save up for it.'

The wedding was quite a festival, with crowds of well-dressed guests and the bride and groom looking slightly dazed as if unable to believe what was happening. There was much gaiety, for it was a wedding of gay colours with three drums being beaten while the couples danced with their backs to one another as they swayed, jumped, clapped hands and sang. The food was excellent, the drinks generous. Cilla and Colin danced and laughed and she was enjoying herself until, as the music paused, a familiar voice made her stiffen with dismay.

'Look who's here! Cilla being introduced to Seychelles' habits.'

Cilla swung round, her hand in Colin's. She felt Colin's fingers tighten round hers. Was he as tense as she was, or was it to encourage her to stand up to this impossible man?

Theo was standing, glass in hand, an amused smile on his face, behind them. By his side was Fiona.

'Glad I met you,' Theo went on, his voice amused. 'Save me phoning you tomorrow, though I must say I didn't expect to see you here.'

Cilla's mouth was dry and a strange trembling seemed to be filling her. Was Theo going to be rude to her? Was he going to order his ward not to go out with Colin? Was he going to make a scene with all these people round them?

'What do you want to tell me?' she asked stiffly.

'Nothing serious.' Theo waved his glass almost patronisingly—at least that was the uncomfortable impression she got. 'I heard from Anthony. He seems worried about you, Cilla.'

She was so surprised it took her a moment before she could speak.

'Worried—about me? But why?'

'Because you can't swim. He's afraid that one day when you're looking for those little crabs you're apparently crazy about, you may slip on the rocks and be swept out in the current and he won't be there to save you.'

Fiona's laugh was shrill and full of contempt. 'Don't tell me it's true! A girl your age who can't swim?'

'And what's wrong with that?' Colin asked, his voice aggressive.

'Nothing, of course,' Theo turned to him. 'Except that my nephew is worried about Cilla and has asked me to teach her how to swim.'

Her hand flying to her mouth, Cilla shook her head. 'I hate swimming . . . I don't want to learn.'

'I'm afraid you've no choice,' Theo told her. 'I've already answered Anthony's letter and promised to teach you.'

Fiona clapped her hands joyfully. 'I know. It will be real fun. I'll ask you both round to our swimming pool and you can teach her there, Theo.'

'There's no reason why a promise to a child should be kept if Cilla doesn't want to learn how to swim,' Colin said angrily.

Cilla caught her breath. Was Theo

deliberately doing this? Baiting Colin in order to make him lose his temper and then having a really big row, perhaps even a fight?

Theo was laughing. 'You're quite wrong, Paine. I knew her aunt Lil very well and she asked me to keep an eye on Cilla. I think it's highly important for her to learn to swim, and learn she will. I'm . . .' he paused, looking at Cilla, his eyes amused, 'I'm sure you'll admit that Aunt Lil would wish me to look after you, Cilla.'

Uncomfortably aware that people were gathering in a circle round them, laughing, joking, talking, perhaps wondering why they were apparently quarrelling, Cilla knew he was just delighting in making her feel a fool. She also realised that he was blackmailing her— quietly threatening to say he was a trustee of the will. The news would flash round the island and Paul would hear and Joanna be so upset.

Somehow Cilla managed to smile. 'If you insist, Theo,' she said lightly. 'Actually Aunt Lil always wished I could swim. It worried her.' She turned to Fiona, and this time it was even, harder to smile. 'How kind of you, it will be much easier in a swimming pool.'

'Be a pleasure,' Fiona told her with a smile. Turning to Colin, Cilla said: 'I've got a headache, Colin. Do you mind if we go?'

'Of course not,' he said eagerly.

'See you . . . some time,' said Theo.

116

How can you avoid it—on such a tiny island?' Fiona said with a laugh.

Cilla's fingers tightened round Colin's as they hurried through the laughing crowd to the quiet sanctuary of his car. He had driven for fifteen miles or so, when he seemed to explode.

'He has no right . . .' he began.

'He . . . he . . .' Cilla burst out. If only she could tell Colin just how much right Theo hadl Then it was as if something snapped inside her and she began to cry. 'He likes to make me look stupid, make all those people laugh at me,' she said in between sobs. 'Why does he have to be so mean? Why must we always fight?'

Colin slowed up the car and parked it on a wide open space that stood high on the coast side, looking down at the moonlit sea as the huge waves came racing in, tossing up the sparkling foam.

He turned and took her in his arms. 'Don't let that . . . that man hurt you. He's not worth worrying about.'

'I felt such a fool. They were all laughing at me,' Cilla wailed like an unhappy child, and Colin kissed her. Slowly, gently, he kissed her cheeks, her eyebrows, the corner of her mouth. Then he turned her head and kissed her on the lips . . . a long kiss.

She lay very still, not returning the kiss nor avoiding it. Even as she lay still, she found herself thinking: 'Is this all a kiss is? Oughtn't one to feel excited, thrilled . . . why, I feel just as I do when Paul kisses me. It's as if he was my brother . . .'

Suddenly they were surrounded by a brilliant light and a car flashed by on the road after turning the corner. The sound of it slowly died away and Colin released Cilla.

'I'm afraid it's serious,' he said, his voice half grave.

'What's serious?' she asked, then wished she hadn't, for his arms tightened round her.

'I'm anti-marriage, but I think I feel differently about you, Cilla. What would you say if I asked you to marry me?'

She could just see his face in the moonlight. He wasn't joking—he was dead serious. She drew a long deep breath. Supposing she did marry Colin? It would solve all the problems. She would get the money and give Joanna her half; she and Colin would be happy together and Theo's taunting words would mean nothing.

But did she love Colin? She liked him very much. She was always happy with him. They never quarrelled, but . . .

That one little word: *But.*

'I'd have to think, Colin,' she told him.

'Okay.' He sounded relieved. 'I'm a patient man.'

He walked with her to Joanna's house after he had driven there, then stooped and kissed her.

'Think about it, Cilla. It means a lot to me,' he said, and strode away towards the car.

Joanna and Paul were out. The house very quiet. Cilla went to bed, but not to sleep. Colin loved her. If she married him, all their problems would be solved—that was, if she could get Peter Kent's consent and also Theo's. Yet what had they against Colin? If she saw another solicitor, perhaps?

Why had Theo suggested such cynical, cruel things? First that Paul might have murdered her . . . and then that Paul had planned this marriage so that he could get Aunt Lil's money. Theo had a cruel, mean mind. If only Aunt Lil had known the sort of man Theo was, she would never have made him a trustee.

CHAPTER ELEVEN

Cilla was eating her breakfast alone as usual when she heard the car come. In a few moments Theo had walked in. He stood in the doorway, tall in his white suit, his face stiff and cold.

'Nearly finished?' he asked curtly. 'I want to talk to you, but I haven't got long.'

'I . . . I won't be a moment,' she said, then wondered why she should automatically do everything he demanded. He had a nerve!' I haven't finished my breakfast,' she added defiantly.

He jerked out a chair and sat down. 'Okay, not that hurry.' He rang the little brass bell and Henrietta came hurrying in, her smile brightening her dark face. 'A cup of coffee, please. Black. Thank you.'

Cilla ate the rest of her breakfast with deliberate slowness. She was not going to jump to attention every time he spoke to her! Unfortunately she was so tense that everything she ate tasted like sawdust! The resentment boiled inside her, building up her anger. He wanted to see her in a hurry? He probably wanted her to ride the horses, for they needed exercise and must have missed it since Anthony left. All Theo did was to make use of her. She was tired of his arrogant selfishness—

dead tired—and he wasn't going to order her around just as if . . .

'Feel like blowing your top, Cilla?' Theo asked, his voice amused. 'Silently this time. What a change!'

She felt her cheeks burn. How could he have known? Was it so obvious?

'I was thinking.'

'That was obvious. Hurry up, now. Your coffee must be cold. Have you forgotten it's there?'

She had! Which didn't help matters, either, so she hastily gobbled down the cold coffee and stood up.

'All right,' she said. 'What do you want me to do this time?' she asked, trying to keep her voice steady, for anger had a horrible habit of making her voice tremble.

He stood up, towering above her, a tall lean man with dark hair and sideboards. A handsome man, but his eyes were cold. And then she saw the same little curl that stood up at the back of his head and that she had noticed that first time they had met—and how absurdly her hand had ached because she wanted to smooth the curl down. Which didn't make sense at all. But her hand still ached!

'Come in the car,' he said curtly.

She followed him outside. He had no chauffeur with him. He drove as if they were going to Victoria, but abruptly turned across the road and parked the car in a large tourists'

121

sightseeing ground that she recognised at once, remembering the night before and the way Colin's car was flooded by the brilliant light of a car that was passing. Had that been Theo's car? Was a lecture about to begin? A warning of a parked car as if she was a teenager or even younger? She was so tired of . . .

Theo's next move found her totally unready, for he stopped the engine, turned to her and swept her in his arms that closed round her like bands of iron. Before she could even struggle his face came down over her, his mouth pressed hard against hers . . .

She stiffened, but there was nothing she could do. She was completely at his mercy and he gave her none as his mouth hardened down on hers brutally.

It was so different from the way Colin kissed her. So . . .

A strange feeling was sweeping through her, a feeling she had never known before. She found herself fighting herself, for she longed to throw her arms round his neck, to press his mouth down, to let her lips return his kiss. Never in all her life had she felt like that . . . never. Why had it to be for a man she hated?

He let her go and she fell back along the seat, limp and exhausted.

'Well?' Theo demanded. There was no affection in his voice, no tenderness.

'Well?' she echoed.

'You were kissing Colin Paine when I drove up last night?'

Some of her vanished strength returned as anger grew. 'And what if I was?'

'Plenty of reasons. That man's a real pain in the neck. He's always . . .'

'It's no business of yours!'

'That's where you're wrong. It is my business. Not from choice, I can assure you.'

'Just because I kissed Colin . . .'

'But did you? You lay like a frozen stick in my arms, stiff as can be as if something revolting was happening.'

A wave of relief swept through her. At least for once he hadn't discovered the truth. The truth that she dared not face up to yet was horribly aware of every moment.

'Why did you kiss me?' she managed to say.

'I wanted to see if you were playing it round. You might have several boy-friends for all I knew. I wanted to find out!'

Her cheeks were hot. 'Find out what?'

He smiled. 'If you were easy.'

'Easy?' she almost shouted, and her hand flew out, aiming for his cheek, but he caught her hand as it flew through the air and his fingers closed tightly round her wrist. 'How dare you! Let me go! You've no right . . . and . . . and was I?'

He laughed, letting go her wrist and tossing her hand down on to her lap. 'On the contrary. I should think my kiss was the first real one you've ever had. You were scared stiff.'

Her cheeks flamed, because he was right on both counts, though one was for a totally different reason. 'And . . . and what if I was? I don't like men who suddenly grab me and . . .'

'Don't you?' he asked, his eyes narrowing, and for a moment she could hardly breathe. Did he know the truth? Had she given it away? If he know . . . oh, then life here would be impossible.

The amusement left his face and he looked stern. 'I must admit I was relieved. I don't want you to get hurt. Steer clear of Colin. He has one idea only—your money. Has he asked you to marry him?'

She nodded, still shaken from the force of Theo's kiss and her fury afterwards.

'You want to?' Theo asked. 'You love him?'

'I . . . I don't know,' she admitted.

'Well, think about it from a different angle,'

Theo told her angrily. 'Colin happens to be one of Paul's best friends. Right? Doesn't that tell you why Colin is buttering you up?'

'I don't understand.'

'In other words, you don't want to. Look, as I told you before, what could be better for everyone than that Colin, who's always in and out of jobs, should marry you? Paul would get Joanna's half and Colin would take over yours. Very convenient. It stinks of Paul.'

'That's not true. Paul wouldn't be like that. Colin isn't just . . .' said Cilla, her voice rising.

'How dare you say such a horrible thing I Colin loves me. He keeps telling me so.'

'A good actor! Or are you too stupid to see the truth? Paul is after your money, and so is Colin.'

Cilla was so angry she fumbled for the car door handle.

'Where are you going?' Theo asked.

'I want to get as far away from you as I can,' she said angrily. 'If I want to marry Colin, I will.'

Theo's hand caught hold of her wrist. 'You can't. Peter Kent thought you'd had enough shocks, so he left out one bit until a more suitable moment. That moment has come. If you marry before you're thirty, you must only marry a man one of the trustees approves of. Write to Peter and ask him if you can marry Colin. Peter knows him, too. Colin worked for me at one stage—nothing but troubles. Peter had to cope with him, he won't have forgotten.'

'I don't believe it,' Cilla said angrily. 'You just dislike everyone I like. If only Aunt Lil could see you now—a fine trustee, I must say! Mocking me, making me look a fool in front of people, trying to spoil everything I do. Colin and I are good friends and I trust him . . .'

Theo had started the engine. 'In other words, you don't trust me,' he said.

She stared at him. 'No . . . I don't,' she said angrily.

'I see.' He smiled. 'I must get you home, as I'm expecting a phone call,' he added casually as if they had not been fighting.

Neither spoke as he drove her back to Joanna's house and when he stopped the car, Cilla got out without a word and almost ran to the house.

As usual Theo seized his chance. 'Mind you don't trip!' he shouted.

Cilla didn't look round, but she did trip, almost stumbling into the house, running along the corridor to her bedroom. Once inside she held her hands to her face as she faced up to the truth. The truth she didn't want to admit—yet the truth that every bone in her body knew and regretted.

How could you love a man you hated so much? she asked herself. Yet that was the truth. Theo's kiss had told her the truth, and the truth was something you could not deny.

That afternoon when Joanna asked questions about the wedding, Cilla had to be careful. Whatever happened no one must know the truth. So she told Joanna about Theo's teasing because she couldn't swim and Fiona's suggestion he should teach Cilla at their swimming pool.

'She just wants to see me make a fool of myself. Everyone was listening, standing round us and laughing.'

Joanna looked uncomfortable. 'Can't you swim yet?' she asked.

Cilla shook her head. 'I'm scared stiff of my face going under water. I don't know why, but I got terribly teased and in trouble at school. This was Anthony's doing. I know he was always worrying in case I slipped on the rocks, so he asked his uncle to teach me.'

'Rather sweet of him.'

'Of Anthony, yes—of Theo, no,' Cilla said bitterly. 'His whole idea was to make me look a fool.'

'Of course Fiona enjoyed the opportunity.'

'She made the most of it. Colin was angry. I was afraid they were going to have a big row.'

'It seems very mean of Theo,' commented Joanna.

'He is mean . . . horribly mean,' Cilla said, and to her dismay found her voice was unsteady and she was near tears. 'I've got a headache—the air is terribly humid. I think I'll go and lie down for a while.'

'Good idea. It is very humid today,' Joanna agreed, staring after her sister, a little puzzled.

But Cilla had gone and was soon lying on her bed, her face buried in her hands as she tried to work out what to do next. Whatever happened, no one—least of all Theo—must ever know that she loved him.

CHAPTER TWELVE

The exceptionally humid air acted to help Cilla, since she could pretend it made her feel exhausted and so spent the next week mostly in bed. Joanna was sympathetic, and when Colin phoned she explained that Cilla was not used to this kind of climate and not fit to go out dancing or to dinner. Colin accepted it and Cilla spent hours lying on her bed, her mind whirling round and round as she tried to make sense of her own behaviour.

How could you love a man you hated?

How could she be so stupid as to let herself fall in love with a man like Theo?

Was she really in love with—should she say, did she really love?—Theo? Had her reaction to his kiss been a mere chemical reaction? Marriage based entirely on a sexual aspect could surely not succeed. Wouldn't she be happier with Colin? Colin who loved her dearly, who was so gentle, with whom she could spend hours and neither of them say a cruel word? Surely that was a far better background to a happy marriage? But when you marry, did you have to ask yourself all these questions? Surely you should know the answers without asking the questions. When you loved . . .

Suddenly the rain came and Cilla's excuse

ceased to exist, so she got up, having made up her mind to go to Victoria, and find a solicitor to ask his advice about Aunt Lil's will and to discover if a 'condition' could prevent her from marrying without one of the trustees' approval. She did not believe it. Theo was merely tricking her . . . Also she would ask the solicitor to write to Peter Kent and find out just how long Aunt Lil had said she must stay on the island, for the sooner she left it, the better . . .

Yet, she thought, she had grown to love the island and the way of living. She could not see herself back in London, living in a flat in Gloucester Road, queueing up for the bus in the rain, battling with a crowd on the underground, going to that office day after day after day . . . Never to see Theo again . . .

She turned away from the window, her eyes smarting as the tears flooded them.

'Face the truth,' she told herself sternly. 'You must go. You have no choice.'

Joanna was still asleep as she always slept until about twelve o'clock, so Cilla went out to her sports car, rubbing her hand over the side of it. She would miss this car. Funny how fond of a car you could get, and Joanna would sell it and buy another.

Deciding to go straight into town and find a good solicitor, Cilla looked through the pockets on the side of the car and was startled to find a silk scarf. It could only be Theo's.

Why, it must have lain there for ages-she could not remember when last Theo was in her car.

Theo was quite capable of accusing her of having stolen it. What a joke he could make it, she thought. Joanna's was not far from his house and he was probably out, so she decided to take the scarf over. She could give it to Ermyntrude.

As she drove up towards the house she loved so much, she wished she had not come, for it only made it all so much more painful. Whatever happened she didn't want to see Theo.

She drove round the back of the house, taking the scarf and walking with the dogs jumping up at her, to the kitchen. It was empty, so she walked through into the hall and Ermyntrude came running, her face frightened.

'It is God's answer to my prayer,' the Creole maid said. 'He is so ill I am afraid. I know not what to do.'

'What's the trouble, Ermyntrude?' Cilla had grown to know and like the Creole girl during Anthony's stay and was startled at the fear in Ermyntrude's face.

'It is *him*,' Ermyntrude wailed. 'He not eat or get-up for four days. He run with water. He not speak—he just toss around.'

Cilla knew who *him* must be, yet she could not believe it. Theo—that strong arrogant creature—ill? It didn't make sense. Obviously

130

the girl was really frightened, and living on the island she must often see people suffering from fever, so surely . . . ?

'You sent for the doctor, Ermyntrude?'

'No—I afraid. Him . . . he and the doctor not good friends. Him has no time for the doctor, he says.'

'That's nonsense. When you're really ill . . . I'd better see him. Take me to his room, Ermyntrude.'

Together they walked down the corridor and the Creole girl opened the door and stood back so that Cilla could walk through.

But her legs seemed to have lost their strength for a moment as she stood there, unable to believe what *she* saw.

Theo, in white shortie pyjamas, was lying down on top of his bed, if the tossing and turning could be called 'lying down'. He was moaning and groaning and the sweat was pouring down his face, his eyes were closed.

'Theo!' Cilla exclaimed, horrified, and turned to Ermyntrude. 'Get a flannel from the bathroom, soak it in cold water and wipe his face.' Ermyntrude looked terrified, so Cilla smiled. 'Look, I'm going to phone the doctor at once, so get a bowl of ice-cold water and a flannel and have it ready for me.'

'*C'est bien*,' Ermyntrude, looking relieved, said.

Cilla got through on the phone with surprising speed. The doctor was out, at the hospital. So she phoned the hospital. The doctor was busy—in the operating theatre.

'But he must come,' Cilla said, her voice desperate. 'Mr Randall is terribly ill, unconscious.'

'I will tell the doctor. He will come as soon as he can.'

'I mean it . . . he's seriously ill,' Cilla said again.

'But of course, *mademoiselle.* I will tell the doctor at once,' the oily voice promised.

Cilla hung up. She could do no more, yet was that enough? How long did an operation take?

Back in the room with the twisting tossing body on the bed, she carefully wiped his face with the cold cloth, feeling sick with fear. What ought she to do? If only she knew more

Looking at his grey contorted face with the sweat running down in small rivulets, she had never felt so useless. Suppose . . . just suppose Theo died . . .

It was as if a hand gripped her throat, stopping her from breathing. If Theo died . . .

It seemed hours that Cilla stood there, bathing the unconscious face, praying that she was doing the right thing, blaming herself for never having learned first aid. What was the illness? she wondered. She asked Ermyntrude, who stood hovering in the doorway, her face streaked with fear, but the Creole girl didn't know either. Cilla wondered if she should ring

132

Joanna—but she would still be asleep; besides, it was unlikely that Joanna would know anything about this kind of illness.

'Wet his face,' Cilla said to the Creole girl, who came forward, her eyes huge with fear. 'I must ring the doctor again.'

The same oily persuasive voice answered her. 'But of course the doctor has been told. He is a busy man and . . .'

'I want to speak to him. I must speak to him. I insist on speaking to him!' Cilla's voice rose furiously. 'Do you realise Theo might die?' she almost screamed. 'If you don't put me through to the doctor I'll . . .'

She heard the unknown woman sigh heavily. 'All right, I will tell the doctor that you wish to speak to him. What name may I give?'

'Cilla Askew. I'm a neighbour of Mr Randall's . . .'

'Miss Askew?' The oily voice brightened. 'Oh, you must be . . .

'Yes, I am,' Cilla shouted angrily. 'I'm the sister whose aunt left her money to . . .'

'I'm sorry, Miss Askew, I didn't mean to offend,' the woman said politely. 'Hold on and I will put you through to the doctor.'

There was a crackle and then a deep voice spoke. 'Miss Askew? I understand you are almost hysterical about something?'

It was a pleasant voice, friendly but slightly amused.

'So would you be hysterical if you could see

133

Theo Randall,' Cilla said angrily. 'Look, he's unconscious and I think he's dying and . . .' Her voice stopped, for it was shaking, and her eyes smarted again. If only she could make them understand!

'Theo? Theo Randall? Don't tell me he's ill. Probably it's a hoax and you've fallen for it.'

'Listen, Doctor,' Cilla said, her voice quiet now as she fought for control of herself, 'I know Theo is normally healthy, but he hasn't eaten anything for days and he's unconscious —tossing about on the bed, moaning, the sweat running down his face. I don't know what to do!'

'I'll be with you in twenty minutes,' the doctor said, and she heard the click as he replaced the receiver.

She put down the phone, trembling, for the doctor's immediate response had shown how very ill Theo must be. But at least the doctor was coming.

She hurried along to Theo's bedroom and took over from Ermyntrude.

'The doctor is coming,' she announced.

'It is good. I make some coffee?'

'I'd rather have a cold drink with lots of ice.'

'It shall be,' Ermyntrude said, and turned away, looking relieved at having an excuse to escape.

To Cilla it was an endless twenty minutes as she bathed the sweating face and looked at the man before her, tossing and turning, moaning and groaning, so very different from the man she . . . hated. But that was no longer the truth. This was the man she loved . . . and there was nothing she could do about it.

Then she heard the sound of the bell—a man's voice and Ermyntrude's voice, and in a few moments the doctor was there.

At the time she hardly noticed him—just the man who had come to save Theo's life.

'Go and relax,' the doctor ordered. 'Leave Randall to me.'

'I didn't know what to do . . . I don't know what's wrong with him . . .'

The doctor's hand was gentle on her arm as he took her to the door and put her outside. 'You've done very well. Don't worry. Go and sit down and have a drop of brandy. I'll come along as soon as I've finished.'

'Finished?' she echoed.

He smiled and she saw for the first time just how sun-tanned his face was, in real contrast to the fairness of his hair.

'An injection that'll calm him down. Nothing to worry about.'

A wave of relief went through her and she obeyed, her legs absurdly shaky as she went to sit down. Ermyntrude came hurrying.

'The doctor says some brandy,' Cilla told her.

'It is good. I will get it. Your legs, you put them up,' Ermyntrude said briskly, finding a small chair and fussing over Cilla.

As she sipped the fluid that stung her throat and then seemed to circulate comfortingly down her body, causing her stomach nerves to relax, Cilla closed her eyes, resting her head on the back of the chair. There was no doubt now—if there had been any doubt at all—that she loved Theo. Loved him far too much.

She must have dozed, for she woke suddenly when the doctor walked in, sat down opposite her.

'He'll be all right,' he said briefly.

Cilla stared at him. 'You're sure?'

The tall thin blond man smiled. 'Quite sure. It's an attack of a tropical fever. He's had several attacks before, but he gets so furious with his own weakness that he won't send for me. Not exactly an easy man,' the doctor said with a laugh.

'And that's no lie,' Cilla laughed as she felt the wave of joyous relief sweep through her. Theo was all right. There was no need to fear.

'Let me introduce myself,' the doctor said. 'David Temple.' He held out his hand and shook Cilla's. 'And you?'

'Cilla Askew.'

'Oh yes . . .'

Cilla's cheeks burned. 'Of course you've heard of me,' she said, her voice defiant. 'I'm the sister who stole Joanna's share.'

He laughed. 'You know what life is like in a place this size. They've got nothing to do but gossip and what they don't know they invent.

No, what I heard about you was that you'd looked after Theo's nephew, a boy you'd flown out from England with and that Fiona thought you'd kidnapped.'

'You know her?' she asked.

'Who doesn't?'

'How is it we haven't met?'

'Because I only got back yesterday. I've been on leave, flew over to Scotland to see my parents.'

'Then if it had been yesterday, I wouldn't have got you?' Cilla sounded dismayed.

Chuckling, he shook his head. 'No, but there was someone in my place. I'm glad you got me, as I know Theo.'

'The maid said you were not friends.'

'Who can always be friends with Theo?' David asked. 'He's a generous man. Has contributed a lot for the hospital, but he expects everything to be done his way. That's where we fight. He may be a first-rate architect, but he doesn't know what a medico needs. It takes some doing to prove to him that his ideas, while perfect, are not practical. How do you get on with him?'

'I . . . we . . .' She was taken aback by the question, but soon recovered and managed to smile. 'Oh, we fight all the time.'

David stood up. 'Good to hear of a lass who'll refuse to lick his boots! Theo is a great guy, but there are times . . . Now I must be off, but I'll be sending a nurse down as more injections will be needed, and I'll be in to see him later today.'

Cilla stood up quickly. 'What can I do to help?'

'Actually nothing. If he sweats badly, wipe his face with a cold cloth as you did.' His face was suddenly grave. 'It's a good thing you phoned for me. A few more hours and it might have been too late.'

As she went out to his car to see him off, Cilla shivered despite the heat, for the sky was a cloudless blue again.

David Temple waved goodbye and Cilla went back into the house, wishing the doctor could stay, feeling so helpless if Theo needed help.

She went to Theo's room and stood in the doorway. His body was still, he had stopped moaning, but he was still unconscious, the sweat pouring down his face. She bathed his hot skin, seeing that the little curl of hair had been squashed down by the sweat, and she stroked it gently, trying to make it stand up, but it collapsed.

Sitting by his side, wondering when the nurse would come and how long it would be before Theo was well, Cilla was quite startled when someone stormed into the room.

'What are you doing here? You've no right . . .' the angry girl burst out. It was Fiona! As usual elegantly beautiful in a white trouser suit, her hair elaborately coiled, Fiona's cheeks were bright red with fury. 'Why didn't you ring me and tell me Theo was ill?' she demanded, almost shouting. 'You have no right to be here. I'm the one. As you know, we're very close and soon will be announcing our engagement.'

Cilla stared silently. It was not true, she told herself. Fiona was making it all up.

'Theo is tired of the way you chase him,' Fiona went on. 'Tired to death at the way you make it plain you're after him.'

Unable to help laughing, Cilla saw Fiona's anger deepen. 'I asked you—what are you doing here?' Fiona demanded. 'Theo will be furious!'

Fiona's anger seemed easier to cope with than Theo's, Cilla thought. 'I found one of Theo's scarves in my car, so I brought it over,' she said, pointing to the scarf on the chair.

'Theo's scarf?' Fiona said sneeringly. 'A likely story, but it doesn't work. That's Colin's scarf. I know because I gave it to him last Christmas.'

'Colin's?' Cilla was startled. It made sense, though, for she had driven him in her car quite recently about town. Now why hadn't she thought of Colin? Because Theo ruled her thoughts? The worst part was, Cilla realised, that Fiona would tell Theo and make the most of it, and Theo . . .

Cilla put the damp flannel in the bowl of water. Glancing quickly at Theo, she thought he was not sweating so much as before.

Perhaps the injection was having a good effect. She looked at Fiona.

'A nurse is coming to give injections,' she told her. 'Dr Temple says Theo will be all right.'

'Of course he will, now I'm here. I'm used to nursing this. Now, get out,' Fiona said rudely.

Cilla turned and walked out, down the corridor and to her car. She felt strangely weak and angry—angry with herself for making such a mistake as to take Colin's scarf. She looked down and saw it in her hand. Without realising it, she must have clutched it as she left the room. Fiona would tell Theo about it—and imply that Cilla had deliberately muddled the owner of the scarf in order to use it as an excuse to call on him. How stupid had she been? Cilla thought crossly, then realised something else.

As the doctor had said, if she *hadn't* found Theo so ill, it might have been too late.

CHAPTER THIRTEEN

Cilla drove straight back to Joanna's, only remembering as she drove up in front of the house that she had planned to go to town and find a solicitor so that she could fight Theo. But it was different now. She couldn't do it while Theo was ill.

All was quiet, so Cilla went and lay on her bed, switching on the electric fan that sent a delightful cool air over her. What was she to do? She could imagine the grapevine passing on the words : Cilla was nearly hysterical about it—she had gone to see him with some stupid excuse. Of course he was all right as soon as Fiona got there!

Who had told Fiona? The oily-voiced girl at the hospital? Wondering if she should tell Joanna the truth of what actually happened and let there be a second side of the story?

But Joanna at lunch had a migraine. She looked worried, but kept saying she was all right. The phone bell rang once and she came back to the dining room, looking puzzled.

'I've just heard that Theo is ill—some kind of fever.'

'Yes, I was . . .' Cilla began, but stopped as Joanna ran her hand over her forehead.

'Gee, it's bad this time. Mind if I go back to bed, Cilla?'

'Of course not. I hope it'll be better soon.'
Joanna smiled. 'I hope so, too. I expect Colin
will ring you up as it's cooler.'

'Not much cooler,' Cilla said with a smile.

'You'll get used to it,' Joanna reassured her.
'We all do.'

As Joanna left her, Cilla was thinking that
she would not be on the island long enough to
get used to it! Surely Aunt Lil's conditions had
not been for years here, only months?

Colin did ring later and Cilla went out with
him. He was his usual charming self,
thoughtful, considerate, but asking her if she
had thought about his proposal.

'Of course I have,' she said, turning to smile
at him. The moonlight shone down on them
where they were parked above the coast with
its huge rocks and racing-in waves. 'But I'm
sorry, Colin, I'm very fond of you, but . . .'

'I wish that word "but" had never been
invented,' he sighed. 'It spoils everything.'

Cilla had to laugh. 'I think it's the most
important word in the world. It makes you
think.'

'Perhaps you're thinking too much,' he said.

She turned to him. 'Colin, please! I enjoy
going out with you, we get on well together,
can't we just enjoy being together without
thinking of marriage? At least not for a while.'

He kissed her gently, a kiss that meant
nothing to her. Nothing at all.

'I love you,' he told her, 'so I'll be patient.'

And so started a new phase of Cilla's life. Paul, bad-tempered and tired, bringing more and more work home. Joanna obviously worried about something, for her migraines grew worse and worse, and Colin taking Cilla out, being the good friend she needed but not pestering her. It was hard to hide her interest in Theo's illness, but the grapevine kept them up to date. What puzzled Cilla was that never once did she hear her name mentioned, so it looked as if Fiona had told no one at all, which was rather surprising.

And so the days passed and Cilla could not make up her mind. Marrying Colin would solve many problems, but if Theo was right and she had to have one of the trustees' permission, then she had better write to Peter Kent at once. She could hardly say 'Yes' and then have to tell Colin why she couldn't marry him. So she wrote the letter and going outside on to the shady terrace, found Joanna waiting for her.

'What's wrong with you, Cilla?' she asked. 'These days you look so miserable.'

Cilla felt like saying: 'So do you and Paul', but decided not to as it might be something private.

'I am worried,' she said slowly. 'You see, Colin has asked me to marry him.'

Joanna looked surprised. 'I didn't think he was the marrying kind. Do you love him?'

'That's it.' Cilla sat down and stretched out

143

her legs as she smiled. 'That's the whole point. I can't decide. I like him very much, very much indeed, but . . .' She laughed. 'Poor Colin! He's been so patient and gets quite cross because I keep saying " but".'

'You don't love him?' asked Joanna.

'What is love?' Cilla asked evasively. 'I'm happy with him. We never quarrel.'

'How boring married life would be if you never quarrelled. Making the quarrels up is the sweetest part of it.'

'I hate quarrels,' confessed Cilla.

'Then why do you and Theo quarrel all the time?'

'He does the quarrelling. He's impossible.'

'Talking of Theo, I think we ought to go and visit him,' Joanna said, standing up, looking as beautiful as usual with her red hair and lovely skin.

'Go and see him?' Cilla was startled. 'Why?'

Joanna looked amused. 'Why? Sheer politeness. We're neighbours and old friends and yet we've done nothing to help him in his illness. The least we can do is to go and cheer him up in his convalescence. I hear he's very depressed.'

'Theo? Depressed?'

'Yes, come along. It's the least we can do. I've got some fruit he likes,' Joanna said. 'I'll get it.'

Reluctantly, yet wanting to go at the same time, Cilla led the way to the car. It was a beautiful day, but still very humid. Joanna said little as they drove to Theo's house.

As usual Cilla's heart gave an extra throb as she saw the beautiful—as she thought it—building. One of her handful of dreams, she thought. A dream that had turned into a nightmare.

Theo was sitting on the grass under the huge sunshade. He stood up and waved and the two girls walked across the lawn, Joanna smiling, Cilla trying to look impersonal.

'Well, this is a nice surprise,' Theo said, his usual sarcastic smile hurting Cilla. 'Long time no see. Ermyntrude,' he shouted, 'cold drinks, please. Do sit down, Cilla, your legs look as if they're wobbling.'

They were! Cilla thought as she hastily sat down. If only he didn't see everything!

'This is a real surprise,' Theo went on. 'I began to wonder if I had any friends or neighbours, because no one called to see the poor sick man.' He smiled as he spoke, but there was a tiny thread of bitterness in it.

'We . . . we heard you weren't allowed visitors,' Cilla explained.

Theo turned to stare at her, his eyes suddenly cold. 'Now who would be stupid enough to believe that? I've been longing for visitors. Thanks be, Fiona comes every day, so I'm not completely alone.'

Ermyntrude came out with the tray of glasses and iced water and orange squash. She

145

gave Cilla a quick, rather frightened look that was puzzling. The Creole girl looked for a moment as if she was wanting to speak, but then she turned and almost fled across the grass.

Theo noticed and said : 'I don't know what's the matter with Ermyntrude. She's so different since I've been ill. Crawls around as if she expects me to chop her head off.'

Cilla thought she could imagine how Fiona spoke to Ermyntrude and that was probably the trouble, only she could hardly say so, for it was obvious that Theo thought the world of Fiona.

It became even more obvious as they drank and chatted, for Theo was saying he would have died if Fiona hadn't found him so ill and sent for the doctor.

'I wasn't conscious, but you'd have thought Ermyntrude would have had the sense.'

Cilla opened her mouth, about to say that Ermyntrude had been scared, knowing how much he disliked the doctor.

'And Fiona's been a wonderful nurse,' he went on. 'Of course I had a real nurse, too, but Fiona just sat and bathed my poor hot face.' He chuckled. 'Sounds odd, doesn't it, a man of my age having his face washed!'

'Very kind of her,' Joanna agreed, finishing her glass and smiling. 'And you're really well, now?'

'Just outrageously weak. I was furious when

I got better and leapt out of bed. You would have laughed,' he said, looking challengingly at Cilla, 'if you'd seen me collapse on the floor. My legs were absolutely useless, but they're better now.'

'You've . . . you've seen the doctor?' Cilla asked nervously. It was obvious that Fiona had not told Theo that it was Cilla who had found him and who had sent for the doctor, thus saving Theo's life. On the other hand, it also meant that Fiona had not mentioned the scarf, or accused Cilla of having deliberately lied about the scarf in order to have an excuse.

Theo looked amused. 'I never waste his time if I can avoid it. He came when I was unconscious and once as I was getting better. I don't need to see him. An obstinate bloke, gets on my nerves.'

Cilla longed to say, 'And you get on his with your arrogance,' but luckily she stopped herself in time, since it would have betrayed everything.

Driving home with Joanna, Cilla said, 'Did I tell you that Theo says I can't marry anyone unless he or Peter Kent approves?'

'Good grief, surely not? Isn't that carrying it a bit far?' Joanna asked in a sympathetic voice.

'Personally I don't believe it, so I've written to Peter to ask him. Oh, Joanna, I feel like flying back to England on the next plane and telling the trustees what they can do with their . . . their money.'

147

Joanna's hand flew to her mouth. 'Please don't do that, Cilla.' She turned, her face frightened. 'I didn't want to tell you, but I'm up to my eyes in debt. I knew I was a fool, that I should have had more sense, but somehow I always had a feeling Aunt Lil would die soon and we would inherit all that money, so I could pay the bills. That's why I was so beastly to you when you first came out. I was frightened.'

'Oh, Joanna, how awful! I'm sure there must be some way we can get some money for you. Look, if I can marry Colin, it will solve all our problems.'

'Too big a price for you to pay,' Joanna said, and patted Cilla's hand. 'Don't worry, we'll find a way.'

'Joanna,' Cilla went on, 'Theo made me terribly angry, because he said Paul had introduced Colin to me in order to get the money.'

'Theo said that?' Joanna's cheeks were red. 'How . . . But then Theo just doesn't understand. He's never liked Paul, always seen the worst in him. Theo can't see that all men are efficient, ambitious and hard-working, but in their own way. He loves his work. Paul loathes his—at least this job. No, I'm sure he would never do that. He's *very* fond of you— besides, it isn't the sort of mean thing he'd do.' She clicked her fingers. 'I bet you it was Fiona. She got scared in case you got Theo whom she's determined to get, so she put Colin on

your track. What do you think?' Joanna
finished, laughing and yet somewhat serious.

Cilla looked thoughtful as she drove into
the garden of Joanna's house. 'You could be
right. Fiona's known Colin for years.'

'You're not going to marry him, are you?'

'I don't know. I honestly don't know. If I
can't get Peter's permission I have to wait until
I'm thirty before I can marry whom I like.'

'It's ridiculous,' Joanna said angrily. 'I don't
believe it. I bet they're making it up for some
reason.'

'That's what I think, Joanna. I want to get a
solicitor and ask his advice, because I think
Theo likes power, to order me around and
make me miserable. He certainly succeeds.'

As they walked up to the house, Joanna
tucked her hand through Cilla's arm. 'Don't
worry, Cilla, things will work themselves out.
Just don't rush into things. We'll find a
solution. That's what Paul is trying to do.'

'Is it why he's so irritable and always
bringing work home?'

'Yes, he's doing correspondence studies.
Got some big idea.' She smiled. 'I do hope he
succeeds. It'll just show Theo.'

'I doubt if he'd notice,' Cilla said bitterly.
'The only person Theo sees is himself.'

'My,' Joanna said slowly, gazing at her
younger sister, 'you do hate the poor man!'

Cilla managed to smile. Better, far better for
Joanna to think that than to know the truth.

CHAPTER FOURTEEN

One evening as Cilla dined with Colin, she realised how little she knew about him. According to Theo Colin had once worked for him—and had been dealt with—whatever that meant!—by Peter Kent. Was it in England or on the island? Cilla wondered. Colin had been here for some time, too, according to Joanna and Fiona.

Colin laughed when Cilla pointed this out. 'Why didn't I tell you? I thought you'd be bored. Where do you want me to start?'

'At the beginning. You know all about me, my father dying, us going to live with Aunt Lil who looked after us when our mother died.'

'Okay, you've asked for it,' shrugged Colin.

It was a sad story and made her feel closer to him, for he, too, had lost his mother, but that was when he was born and his father was in the Merchant Navy. 'So I rarely saw him. I was passed from foster-mother to foster-mother. I must have been an awful child. No one wanted me.'

Poor Colin, who had never known what love really was.

But neither had Theo, and she felt no sympathy for him, she realised with a shock. Yet it must have been just as hard to be handed over to a difficult grandfather while

150

your sister went to a grandmother.

When Colin kissed her, his hand running down her arm, she found herself fighting the desire to push him away. Which was ridiculous, because she was fond of him. As he let her go, she shivered.

Alone in her bedroom, she tried as she had so often done to sort things out. She was fond of a man who loved her dearly and would probably make a good husband, yet she *loved* Theo Randall, who had probably never seen her as a woman, just as the young girl she had seen in the portrait he was painting of her.

Shopping in the market one morning, the sun blazing down, the piles of flowers such lovely crimson, purple and deep golden colours that her eyes were drawn to look at them all the time, she almost bumped into Fiona. Cilla's first impulse was to walk by, pretending she had not seen her, but Fiona gave her no chance, grabbing her arm and smiling—a scornful smile.

'Haven't seen you around lately. Been ill?' Fiona asked.

'No,' Cilla said curtly, trying to free her arm, but Fiona's fingers were firm.

'Doesn't Colin take you out any more?' Fiona smiled.

Cilla was frowning. 'Of course he does. We dance most evenings.'

'Where?'

Feeling inclined to tell Fiona to mind her

own business, Cilla shrugged. 'Usually at one of the restaurants.'

'I see. Colin doesn't get invited round like Theo does, but then there is a difference.'

Cilla stiffened, with the swarming crowd of shoppers round them, the women in brightly coloured skirts and blouses, the men in well-cut suits. 'What difference?' she asked.

'One has money, the other none . . . yet!' Fiona added with a smile that Cilla could only describe to herself as malicious. 'Is he chatting you up?'

'Look, I mind my own business, so please mind yours,' Cilla snapped, so angry she could hardly speak.

'I do. I miss Theo very much,' Fiona said with a smile.

'You miss him?' Taken off her guard, Cilla asked.

'Yes, he's gone off again. Didn't he say goodbye to you? How very rude of him,' Fiona added with a smile, then she let go of Cilla's arm and walked away.

Cilla stood still for a moment. Theo had gone? Where? When would he be back? Why hadn't he said goodbye to her?

The questions seemed to be buzzing round in her head.

*   *   *

Sometimes it seemed to Cilla that she would

never get the letter she was waiting for. Surely Peter Kent could have nothing so serious against a man like Colin to make him forbid the marriage? And once she knew she was able to marry him without causing poor Joanna to lose her share of the heritage, then Cilla knew she could—she would *have* to—make her own decision. Did she love Colin enough to marry him?

When at last the letter came it was absurd, but her hands were shaking a little as she opened the envelope. There was a well-typed letter. She read it and felt a surge of relief mixed with disappointment.

'I am afraid Mr Kent is away, but I will ask him to write immediately he returns,' Betty Armitage wrote.

So nothing had changed? Cilla was still in Square One!

There was a sealed envelope as well and as she took it out of the bigger envelope Cilla caught her breath as she recognized Aunt Lil's neat handwriting. Aunt Lil had been a great letter-lover and always answered immediately she received a letter. Cilla's eyes stung as she looked at the well-known handwriting. She had loved Aunt Lil so much, and what had always been so important was the fact that Aunt Lil had loved her and showed her delight when Cilla came home at the weekends.

Surely the letter was to have come on her wedding day, Cilla was thinking—but if that was so, surely Peter's secretary would know that? Perhaps the letter was only to have been kept until a marriage was planned. Suddenly Cilla ached for Aunt Lil's message—it would be a wish for her niece's happiness and it would be so good to read those loving words . . .

It didn't take long to take out the letter and unfold it flat, and Aunt Lil's clear, neat writing was there to be read.

'My very dear Cilla,

'This must be a happy day for you. It is for me. I only wish I could be with you. You are such a dear girl, quiet, unselfish and loving. You deserve a fine husband.

'As you have perhaps guessed, that is why I made my will so complicated. I like and respect Theo Randall and I am hoping that you, by staying on the island and having him as a trustee, may have grown to love him. I am sure he will love you. Maybe I should not play the part of a matchmaker, but your future happiness is so important to me and I feel Theo would make you a very good husband and that you would be a good wife.

'Of course it is quite possible that you have fallen in love with another man. If so, I send my love and good wishes just the same, but I can't help hoping the man who will stand by your side at the altar

154

will be Theo.

'I also hope that perhaps by staying with your sister, it will help you both to understand one another. You are both adults now and no longer quarrelsome children, so perhaps you are good friends. I do hope so.

'All my love to you both.'

Aunt Lil had signed her letter with a flourish. If only it could have been a triumphant one! If only . . .

Cilla went outside on to the shaded terrace. She felt confused. Dear Aunt Lil, she had always loved to organise things or help people to be happy. But if only this time she had left them alone, then all would have been well. She and Joanna would have shared the money and Joanna's debts would have been paid, Cilla thought. She herself would have got a riding school and a lot of dogs, happy as could be, whereas now she had only heartbreak, loving a man who saw her as a six-year-old child.

Joanna came out. 'An interesting letter?' she asked, looking tired and worried.

'Sit down and read this,' said Cilla. 'Aunt Lil, bless her, with the best intentions in the world, got us in this mess. She played a trick on me—that was why the will was so complicated. Read the letter.' She lay back on the canvas chair, held out Aunt Lil's letter. 'I feel so humiliated-as if . . . as if . . . I was a slave being put on show in the market!'

Sitting down, Joanna read the letter. She looked up with a laugh.

'The old darling! She meant well.'

'I know she did—but tricking poor Theo into feeling responsible for me—as if he hasn't enough to do as it is. I can only hope he doesn't know. If only Aunt Lil had just done what we both thought she would . . .'

'You'd never have come out here—we'd never have become good friends and you'd never have met Theo,' Joanna said with a smile.

That was true, Cilla thought. Would it have been better if she had never met Theo? There wouldn't be this pain, but . . .

'I feel very guilty about Aunt Lil,' Joanna said thoughtfully. 'She loved us both, but you were the one who returned the love. Well,' she smiled, 'did Aunt Lil's trick work? Is Theo going to marry you?'

Cilla drew a deep breath. 'Theo marry me? Why, he doesn't even see me!'

'Would you like to marry him?' Joanna asked gently, her eyes worried.

'Me marry Theo?' Cilla laughed, a harsh unnatural sound. 'I wouldn't marry him if he were the last man on earth!'

It was the biggest lie she had ever told and she knew Aunt Lil would be disappointed in her, for Aunt Lil had taught them to tell the truth always. But how could she tell the truth?

156

Not even to Joanna.

The door behind them swung open and Theo's deep voice chimed in.

'How very interesting, Cilla. I must remind you, though, that you have to be asked before you can refuse.'

Cilla turned, startled and angry. Theo always managed to make her look a fool. 'I didn't hear your car,' she said accusingly.

'I rode over,' Theo told her, looking amused. 'The horses need exercise and . . .'

This was Cilla's chance and she wasn't going to lose it. She jumped to her feet, waving the letter in her hand. 'I might have known it! That's why you came to see me,' she almost shouted. 'We only see you when you want something done. You just make use of me!'

He looked amused. 'Too true. I'll be grateful if you do, but you don't have to ride them if you don't want to. I thought you might enjoy it. Pierre says you're a good rider.'

'Fiona told me you were away,' she said accusingly, and then wondered why she had said such a stupid thing. What did it matter to her if he was away or not? Or at least, that was what he must think.

'Fiona!' Theo laughed scornfully. 'She talks a lot of rubbish. I had to visit one of the islands. I was going to ask you if you'd like to come with me, Cilla, but I gathered you refused to go anywhere without Colin Paine, and somehow I didn't fancy him coming

157

along.'

'Why not?' Cilla asked indignantly. 'He's a friend of mine. I like him.'

'So I gather. Heard from Peter Kent?'

'He's on holiday, so I didn't get an answer.'

'Who's the letter in your hand from?' Theo asked, darting forward and snatching it out of her hand.

'You're not to read it!' Cilla shouted, moving forward and trying to get the letter back.

Theo was laughing, holding it just too high for her to reach.

'And why shouldn't I read it?'

'Because it's my letter, and you have no right . . .'

Cilla tried to jump up so she could reach it, but Theo went on laughing and keeping it out of reach. 'Is it a love letter from your beloved Colin?'

'No, it isn't, but . . .'

Joanna chimed in, 'I think he has a perfect right to read Aunt Lil's letter, Cilla. He'll know it wasn't your idea. You've made that pretty plain.'

'All right, but . . . but it's my letter and . . .' Seeing she had lost her case, for Theo was not listening to her, but frowning as he read, Cilla sat down sighing. Would this nightmare never end?

'You shouldn't have read this letter until your wedding day,' Theo said, his voice cold.

'You knew that. Or is today your wedding day?'

'Of course it isn't!'

'I understood you wanted to marry Colin Paine. Have you changed your mind?' Theo asked, looking up from the letter.

Joanna laughed. 'She can't make up her mind. I hope she won't. He's a real womaniser.'

'He is not . . .' Cilla began angrily. Why had Joanna to say such a thing?

'How do you know,' asked Theo, his voice scornful, 'with your poor knowledge of men?' He was reading as he spoke and began to laugh. 'Dear old Aunt Lil! She lived in a dream world, believing that if you were sure something would happen, it must. Well, Cilla, it's up to you. You'll have to wait for Peter's permission.' Suddenly he frowned. 'But why did you open Aunt Lil's letter when you knew it was to be read on your wedding day?'

'I wasn't sure . . . and as Peter's secretary sent it I thought I must be wrong and that I could read it when I knew I . . . I was going to get married.' She stopped speaking, for she saw the lack of belief on his face and she lost control of her temper. 'I wanted to read what she said,' she told him defiantly. 'She was my aunt. I had a right . . .'

He shrugged his shoulders. 'We could argue all day and never agree. I'll be glad if you exercise the horses with Pierre, but if you'd rather not, I'll understand. Goodbye,' he was saying as a car drove down the narrow drive.

Joanna leapt to her feet. 'It's Paul!' Her eyes shining, she began to run across the grass as Paul slid out of his car and ran to meet her. Almost automatically Theo and Cilla followed, Cilla puzzled at Joanna's delight. After all, Paul came home every day.

Paul's face had lost its tired, dejected look. 'I've made it . . . I've made it . . . I've made it!' he chanted as he put his arms round his wife and swung her off her feet.

'Oh, Paul—I knew you would!' Joanna was crying, her face radiant with joy, as she clung to him.

Then Paul saw Theo and frowned, but Theo held out his hand.

'Congratulations, Paul. I heard the news this morning. We'll miss you, but we all wish you well.' He turned to Cilla. 'Your problem is solved. As a trustee I wholeheartedly agree to anything you suggest about Aunt Lil's money. She would have been proud of Paul had she known.'

'But . . . but what's happened?' Cilla felt as puzzled as she sounded.

Paul had one arm round his wife while he was shaking Theo's hand.

'It wasn't easy, Theo. Great news, Cilla. I've got a job in New York, somewhere we wanted to go. A really good job with a promising future. I got it myself, too,' he said happily, like a small boy who had won a silver cup for

160

swimming or some other sport. 'We'll sell the house and go off as soon as possible. I can't believe it!'

Joanna looked at him proudly. 'I knew you would. Working so hard, studying. I just can't wait to see New York. It sounds terrific.'

'It will be,' Paul said happily. 'A dream come true.'

Theo was smiling. Cilla knew he was remembering what she had said about dreams. Joanna and Paul were hugging one another again and Cilla was not wanted, she realised, so she slipped up to the house. Nor was she wanted here, for they would be packing, selling the house and off to America. Theo must have followed her at once, for he caught up with her at the house and took hold of her arm. She stood still, keeping her back turned, afraid that if he saw her face he might learn the truth. It was all she could do to stand still, to fight the trembling that threatened.

'What do you want?' she asked, trying to make the words sound cold and unfriendly.

He took his hand off her arm and she felt horribly alone—as she was alone. Theo would no longer be her trustee, no longer interested in her welfare; she would be out of his life. And out of Joanna's and Paul's, for they had an exciting new life awaiting them and did not need or want a third person. She felt as terribly alone as she had the day she had heard Aunt Lil was dead.

161

Theo's voice was cool and indifferent. 'That's the end of that, Cilla. You can do what you like with your money, which means you don't have to marry Colin, unless you love him. I'll write and tell Peter Kent that everything's all right. I've been checking up on Colin. He hasn't gambled for several years, has worked hard and is a different person. Aunt Lil would be proud of him. So everything is all right. Goodbye,' he added.

There was a finality, a cold sort of dismissal about his voice that made her say quickly:

'Goodbye, and thank you,' before hurrying into the house and the quietness of her bedroom.

She closed the door. Now she could do just what she liked. And she had no idea what she wanted to do.

Which was a lie, she told herself. She loved Theo, she wished he loved her. Here was a dream that would never come true.

CHAPTER FIFTEEN

It was one of the hardest decisions Cilla had ever had to make. Perhaps the happiness of Paul and Joanna made her feel her loneliness more—also the fact that to Theo she meant nothing. No longer his ward—no longer had he responsibilities to look after her. He would be glad to be free of such a burden.

Colin had phoned her.

'Cilla darling! Admit I've been the most patient man in the world. I want my answer tonight. I'll call for you at seven and after dinner you must tell me. I can't go on like this indefinitely.'

'I know, Colin. You've been so good. It's just that I want to be very sure,' Cilla had told him apologetically.

'I agree all the way. However, surely now your little "but" has been wiped out? I hope so. Goodbye,' he had added, and rang off before she could speak.

All that day she had thought, trying to see the good reasons for marrying Colin. He was kind and thoughtful. They never quarrelled. They had the same interests. Surely they could make a happy marriage?

She chose of one of her prettiest dresses that night, a pale lemon yellow, the long skirt slit up on either side. Colin looked elegant too in his white jacket suit.

'Well—' he said, taking her hands in his and smiling, 'as I told you once before, you're delectable, delicious and delightful.'

They held hands as they walked down to the car. The warmth of his hand comforted and reassured her. This was a man who loved her dearly, who would never be cruel to her, never make her feel a fool as Theo enjoyed doing. She smiled at Colin, but he lifted his hand.

'No—I don't want to hear until I can take you in my arms,' he said.

The drive to the restaurant perched above the foam-flecked rocks was pleasant, though they talked little. The dinner was well cooked. Afterwards they danced. Colin danced well, too, she thought, and knew what she had decided as he suggested they left.

He parked the car in their favourite 'tourists' place'. There was a lovely view of the moonlit sea and the palms Cilla loved so much.

Colin turned to her and took her in his arms, holding her close, his hand running down her bare arm, his mouth hard against hers. It was the first time he had allowed passion to take charge and his mouth sought out the warm beauty of her lips.

But she pushed him away. 'No, Colin, no!' she said, shocked at the horror in her voice, yet aware of the sickness she felt. 'I'm sorry,' she whispered, and her voice quivered. 'I'm terribly sorry. I thought I loved you, but . . .'

He let her go. Then sat back, folding his arms and frowning.

'Why . . .' he began, then said: 'It's Theo Randall, isn't it? Fiona told me. She said you said you hadn't given him up.'

'No. I meant I wasn't chasing him as she accused me of doing. It isn't Theo,' she lied. 'Oh, Colin, I am so sorry. I shouldn't have kept you waiting. I am so fond of you, but . . .'

'*But* again!' he almost spat the word out. 'It happens to us all, I suppose. Anyhow, better we should find out before we're married.'

'Oh, Colin, you're such a darling,' Cilla said, the tears smarting her eyes. 'I tried to love you, but . . .'

'That damn word again,' he growled. 'I'd better take you home.'

They hardly spoke as he drove back. He walked across the lawn with her to the house.

At the door she said again : 'You're such a darling, Colin. I am sorry.'

He kissed her cheek lightly. 'So I am. Goodbye.'

Cilla waited while he walked back across the lawn. But he did not look round. She watched the car drive away and then went into the house.

Joanna was alone, sprawled on the couch in a grass-green kaftan.

'Hi—you're back early,' she said with a smile. 'What's wrong?'

'I . . . I just told Colin I'm sorry but . . .' Cilla began.

'Don't look so miserable. Colin will recover.'

'I know.' Cilla felt even worse because actually she had been feeling sorry for herself and not for Colin! She was selfishly thinking of her own future. Colin was such a darling, but . . .

'What made you know? I was so afraid you were going to marry him,' Joanna asked.

Cilla kicked off her shoes and curled up in an armchair. 'I know it's going to sound daft, but it was the way he kissed me.'

'He'd kissed you before?' Joanna sounded startled.

'Of course, but quite differently. This time it was . . . well . . .'

'Passionate?' Joanna teased, but her eyes were sympathetic. 'It has to be the right one for that, Cilla.'

'Yes, I suppose so.' Cilla was thinking of Theo's kiss, the harshness, the violence, the thrill.

'Where's Paul?' she asked quickly to change the subject.

'Theo is throwing a stag party. It seems he's going away before we do. All the men have gone, but not the wives.' Joanna laughed, but the words hit Cilla with surprising force.

A stag party? Surely a man had that before he was married? Was Theo marrying Fiona

166

then, after all?

'What are you going to do, Cilla? I know you love the island, but you won't stay here after we're gone, will you? Or why not buy our house and run it as a holiday home for children?' Joanna smiled, but Cilla thought of it gravely, for it might be an idea.

She loved the Islands and had no desire to go back to Gloucester Road and rainy bus stops—but the plain truth was, she told herself gravely, she really wanted to stay in the Seychelles because Theo was here.

But for how long would he be? Fiona hated the islands and wanted to see the world, according to Colin. And when they were there on the islands how could Cilla endure the misery of seeing the man she loved married to another woman? Wouldn't it be more sensible to leave? But did one always do the sensible thing?

'I should go back to England if I were you,' Joanna said gently. 'You've always wanted a riding school and then you can visit us. Wait until we've settled down and come and meet your niece.'

'Niece? Are you pregnant? Oh, how marvellous!' Cilla said eagerly.

Joanna laughed. 'We're thrilled, but she has chosen rather the wrong moment. You won't go rushing off, will you? I hoped you'd help me sort things out and pack. The doctor said I mustn't get overtired.'

'Of course I will. Just think, I'm going to be an auntie!' Cilla said happily.

*   *   *

As the days passed, and the trunks were packed and with some furniture freighted, other stuff was sold until at last the house was empty and Cilla was saying goodbye to Joanna and Paul at the airport. The days had flashed by—or so it seemed to Cilla—and after they had gone she went out in her car, which she was going to sell, for a farewell drive round the island. She had booked her flight to Heathrow but was spending the night at a hotel in Victoria. She wanted a last-minute look at this island where she had been both happy and sad; where she had lived in such totally different ways; where she had fallen in love and lost.

As she drove slowly up the road that wound round the mountains she looked hungrily at the beauty of the purple flowers on the creepers that seemed to cling to the trees and everything else they could clutch. It was as if everything had turned out in its most beautiful to say farewell. Never had she seen so many birds—with their lovely colours, some with their little red bodies and golden breasts. Never had she seen so many cheeky little monkeys who swung from branch to branch, chattering as if singing a song of farewell. As she stopped to gaze down at the ocean with its lovely colours, Cilla felt very near tears.

Anthony had asked her what was love. She had not known, then, but now she knew. Love was not the romantic happiness feeling you read about. Perhaps to a few, but not to her. Love meant a curious mixture of love and hate. Love meant a dismal loneliness that seemed to swamp you, a feeling of despair and helplessness. You loved and he didn't. Could there be anything more painful, more tragic? Was this how Colin had felt? she wondered.

She drove back to the town and went to the garage that was buying her car. Then she went to the hotel. How awful it was to be in a hotel alone. She felt everyone was staring at her, wondering who she was and why she was alone. Was she going to go through life alone?

Could she ever love another man as she loved Theo?

Feeling restless, she wandered down the main street past the market that was always bright with food and fruit and shoppers in bright clothes. A car drove by and caught Cilla's attention. It was a purple car. She knew whose it was—Fiona's!

Fiona was driving. She waved to Cilla and smiled. Cilla waved—her hand stopping up in the air as she saw who it was sitting by Fiona's side. Colin! He had not seen her, he was looking the other way. The car passed and Cilla stood very still. Had Colin recovered so quickly? Had he ever really loved her? It was something she would never know.

Colin had seemed so sincere, so heartbreakingly sad as they said goodbye, yet already he was out with Fiona. Cilla wondered if she could recover as fast. Somehow she doubted it.

She could not forget Theo. She was trying, so hard. But she had only to shut her eyes to see his face with that square chin, the stubborn mouth, the dark eyebrows, the little curl of hair on the back of his head that refused to lie down.

Back in the hotel, she decided to have an early night. Not that she got to sleep any earlier, for she spent most of the evening at the screened window, feeling the refreshingly cool air on her face, looking at the lights of the town and the small twinkling lights from the houses on the mountainsides, mostly hidden by the palm trees. How could she leave the beauty? she wondered. How go back to England to the rain and the cold and the crowds? But go she must. She knew that.

In the morning she was driven to the airport. She went to the counter with her ticket. The girl in charge frowned.

'I'm afraid your ticket has been cancelled,' she said.

'Cancelled?' Cilla was startled. 'But that's impossible. I certainly didn't cancel it.'

'I'm very sorry, but your place has been taken. At the moment, we're very packed.'

'But I want to go today,' Cilla said.

'I'm very sorry, but today we are booked up completely. So we are tomorrow. It's a bad time to book.'

'I know. That's why I booked early.'

'Well, I'm very sorry indeed,' the girl said again.

'But your ticket was definitely cancelled and someone on our waiting list got it. I'm afraid there's nothing we can do to help you.'

'Who cancelled it?' Cilla asked angrily.

Who on earth would cancel it? Unless it was one of Fiona's funny jokes. But why should she do such a thing? There was no point in it.

'I'm afraid I don't know,' the girl apologised. 'I wasn't on duty.'

'Can I book here?' asked Cilla.

'We prefer you to book at the town office,' the girl told her.

Bewildered, Cilla got herself driven back to the hotel. Here she was luckier. Her room hadn't been taken yet, so her luggage was carried up and she followed in a lift, after a very welcome cup of coffee.

As she opened the unlocked door, she stood still in the doorway, shocked into a stiffness that made it hard to breathe.

Theo was sitting in the armchair, his legs thrown over the arm, a pipe in his mouth as he read a newspaper. He must have heard the door, for he turned his head, put down his paper and smiled.

171

'Well,' he drawled.

'Well—what?' she asked, closing the door, leaning against it.

'How did you get on? At the airport, I mean?'

'My ticket was cancelled . . .' she began, and stopped. 'How did you know?'

He smiled. 'Because I cancelled it.'

'You did? But why?'

He stood up and came towards her. She had closed the door. Now she backed against it, but Theo went on moving towards her.

'Why didn't you tell me that *you* saved my life?' he asked.

'I . . . I . . .' she stammered.

'You did, didn't you? You found me tossing and turning, unconscious on my bed. It was you who sent for the doctor and washed my sweating face with cold water. Right?'

'Yes.' Why was he bringing this up, and what had it to do with cancelling her flight?

'Why didn't you tell me? Why did you let Fiona make me believe she was the one?'

'She told me to get out. That you were going to marry her. Then . . . then . . .' Cilla's cheeks burned, 'I made a stupid mistake. I found a scarf in my car and thought it was yours. That . . . that was my excuse for coming over to see you. Fiona said it was Colin's scarf and I had made it up. I didn't want you to . . . to . . .'

'Think you were chasing me?' He smiled.

'That was the last thing I'd accuse you of.'

'How did you find out?' Cilla leant against the door, very aware of his tall, broad-shouldered body, of his face so near hers.

'Ermyntrude told me. When I said you were going back to England she burst into tears and said you were a good lady and she must tell me the truth. It seems Fiona told Ermyntrude that I must not know you'd come over, because I would be very angry with you and I would also sack Ermyntrude. She said you'd been very worried for me. Were you?' he asked quietly, his eyes bright as he watched her mobile, self-betraying face.

'Of course I was. You were terribly ill.'

'The doctor said I would have died. Why did you bother to save my life when you were constantly telling me you hated me?'

'I didn't . . . I mean . . . well, we always seemed to fight and . . . Why did you cancel my plane flight?'

His hands were on her shoulders, running down her arms. Cilla shivered with joy, but tried to keep her face calm.

'I'm still your trustee, still here to protect you,' he said in the pompous voice she had once hated but now loved. 'I think it would be a mistake to go back to London. After all, I did promise Aunt Lil to keep a eye on you.'

'I heard . . . I heard you had a stag party. So you are going to marry Fiona?'

'I'm getting married, but not to Fiona.' His

arms were round her now, she could feel his breath on her cheek as he spoke.

'Then who?' she gasped.

He smiled. 'You—if you'll have me,' he told her.

Her mouth fell open and he closed it gently with his fingers. When he released her lips, she whispered, 'What did you say?'

'Something wrong with your ears?' he teased. 'If you'll have me. Is it true what your sister says? She rang me last night and told me I was a fool, because she knew I loved you. She told me the time of the plane you were catching, so first thing this morning I cancelled your booking. She told me we were two idiots and that we seemed to find it impossible to communicate.'

'Joanna told you?' Cilla said slowly, remembering the previous evening when Joanna had asked her to run outside and get something from the garage. It must have been then that she phoned Theo.

Theo let her go and turned away. He brought out from behind the bed a large square parcel done up in brown paper. He removed the paper and held it for her to see.

It was the painting of herself that Anthony had shown her. But it was different. The girl with the long dark hair no longer looked so young. She had laughing eyes and an amused mouth. She was no longer a child. She had become a woman—young, but nevertheless a

174

woman.

'That's how I see you, Cilla. You always snapped at me and I was fool enough to believe you disliked me. Remember the way you nearly bit my head off when I came over to ask you to exercise the horses? It was just an excuse to get you to my house.'

'I thought you were just making use of me.'

'I love you. Do you love me?' he asked, and suddenly she was in his arms, his mouth on hers as he carried her to the armchair, sat down and held her close. His mouth demanded her love. Cilla lay with her eyes closed, her mouth responding to his, her arms round his neck as she gently pulled the little curl.

The kiss of love, she thought happily.

'On our honeymoon, we'll call in and see Anthony, and later on, Paul and Joanna. You won't mind travelling everywhere with me?'

'I don't mind where we go so long as we're together.'

'That makes two of us,' he said, and kissed her again.

'I was thinking we must give the cats some money,' Cilla said dreamily.

Theo laughed. 'I guessed you'd say that. How happy Aunt Lil must be!'

We hope you have enjoyed this Large Print book. Other Chivers Press or Thorndike Press Large Print books are available at your library or directly from the publishers.

For more information about current and forthcoming titles, please call or write, without obligation, to:

Chivers Large Print
published by BBC Audiobooks Ltd
St James House, The Square
Lower Bristol Road
Bath BA2 3SB
UK
email: bbcaudiobooks@bbc.co.uk
www.bbcaudiobooks.co.uk

OR

Thorndike Press
295 Kennedy Memorial Drive
Waterville
Maine 04901
USA
www.gale.com/thorndike
www.gale.com/wheeler

All our Large Print titles are designed for easy reading, and all our books are made to last.